Praise for Jennifer

Standalone

'A drum-tight sense of suspense and sexual tension' *Publishers Weekly*

'Sizzling, forbidden romance and non-stop action make *The Return* an addictive read. Sign me up for the sequel – I am now officially a Seth-a-holic!' Jeaniene Frost, *New York Times* bestselling author

The Lux series:

'An action-packed ride that will leave you breathless and begging for more' Jus Accardo, author of *Touch*

'Powerful. Addictive' *Winter Haven Books*

'A thrilling ride from start to finish' *RT Book Reviews*

'Witty, refreshing and electrifying' *Shortie Says*

'Fast-paced and entertaining . . . I couldn't put this one down' *YA Fantasy Guide*

The Covenant series:

'Oh my Gods! Wow! Jennifer L. Armentrout is such an amazing writer; my heart is still beating hard against my rib cage' *Book Gossips*

'I am completely hooked on Jennifer Armentrout's Covenant series' *Love is Not a Triangle*

'A great blend of action, drama, and romance . . . simply amazing from beginning to end' *The Reading Geek*

'All the romance anyone would ask for, plus a whole lot of action and suspenseful drama as well' *The Revolving Bookcase*

'Ramps up the action, drama and suspense without ever losing a step' *Dreams in Tandem*

Jennifer L. Armentrout lives in West Virginia. All the rumors you've heard about her state aren't true. Well, mostly. When she's not hard at work writing, she spends her time reading, working out, watching zombie movies, and pretending to write. She shares her home with her husband, his K-9 partner named Diesel, and her hyper Jack Russell Loki. Her dreams of becoming an author started in algebra class, where she spent her time writing short stories . . . therefore explaining her dismal grades in math. Jennifer writes Adult and Young Adult Urban Fantasy and Romance.

Find out more at www.jenniferarmentrout.com
Follow her on Twitter@JLArmentrout
or find her on
Facebook/JenniferLArmentrout

Also by Jennifer L. Armentrout
and available from Hodder:

The Covenant Series
Daimon (novella)
Half-Blood
Pure
Deity
Elixir (novella)
Apollyon
Sentinel

The Lux Series
Shadows (novella)
Obsidian
Onyx
Opal
Origin
Opposition

Standalone Titles
Cursed
Don't Look Back
Unchained (Nephilim Rising)
Obsession
The Return

The Gamble Brothers Series
Tempting the Best Man
Tempting the Player
Tempting the Bodyguard

JENNIFER L. ARMENTROUT

Tempting the Player

A Gamble Brothers Novel

HODDER

Tempting the Player first published in eBook in the United States of America in 2012 by Entangled Publishing, LLC

This paperback edition first published in Great Britain in 2015
by Hodder & Stoughton
An Hachette UK company

1

A CIP catalogue record for this title is available from the British Library

Paperback ISBN 978 1 473 61596 0
eBook ISBN 978 1 444 79852 4

Typeset by Hewer Text UK Ltd, Edinburgh
Printed and bound by Clays Ltd, St Ives plc

Hodder & Stoughton policy is to use papers that are natural, renewable and recyclable products and made from wood grown in sustainable forests. The logging and manufacturing processes are expected to conform to the environmental regulations of the country of origin.

Hodder & Stoughton Ltd
Carmelite House
50 Victoria Embankment
London
EC4Y 0DZ

www.hodder.co.uk

Chapter One

As Bridget Rodgers stared at the old meat-packing warehouse, she kept seeing flashes of the movie *Hostel* in her head. According to her friend, the invite-only, highly gossiped about Leather and Lace club was the place to be. But from the cemented-over windows and graffiti-sprayed exterior walls, in what were probably gang symbols, plus the dim flickering light from the nearby lamppost, Bridget figured most patrons of this club ended up on missing persons posters or on the evening news.

"I can't believe I let you talk me into this, Shell. We're probably going to become some perverted rich man's victim by midnight." Bridget straightened the thick leather belt around the waist of her dress. The belt was purple, of course, and her sweater dress a deep red. Her signature look was a bit gaudy, but at least it would help the police identify her body later.

Shell passed her a droll look. "You don't even want to know what I had to do to get an invite to this club." She waved the business card–sized paper in front of Bridget's face. "We're going to have fun doing something different. Boo on the local watering holes."

For all the hoopla surrounding Leather and Lace, one would think it would be in a better location than Foggy Bottom. With the creepy, unsightly look to it and the fog rolling in every night, it seemed doubtful the place catered to the rich and powerful in DC.

The club had become sort of an urban legend, and the name probably had something to do with it. Leather and Lace. Seriously? Who thought that was a good idea? Supposedly, it was a sex club. A means of hooking up people with "mutual interests," like Match.com for the sexually wild or something, but Bridget didn't really believe it. And if it was, oh well. In reality, all clubs and bars catered to sex in one way or another. It was why half the single people went out on the weekend.

It was why she used to go out on the weekend.

"Come on, get the sourpuss look off your face," Shell said. "You need something fun and new. You *need* to de-stress."

"Getting drunk—"

"And hopefully getting laid," Shell added with a wicked grin.

Bridget's laugh sent puffs of small white clouds into the air. "That's so not going to fix my problems."

"True, but they will definitely take your mind off them."

She did need some good old-fashioned stress relief, though. As much as she loved her job and really wanted to go cry in the corner at the thought of finding something else, it wasn't covering her bills—namely the student loans—that were taking a huge chunk out of her monthly income. She'd come to loathe when her phone rang, and it was an eight hundred number.

Sallie Mae was a freaking vulture.

She sighed as she glanced back at the building. That *was* a gang sign. "So how did you score an invite to this place?"

"It's really not that exciting," Shell said, frowning at the card she held.

"All right," Bridget said, squaring her shoulders as she turned to her friend. The shorter girl was shivering in her skintight black mini and Bridget smiled. Sometimes having extra padding had its benefits. Early October air was chilly, but her knees weren't knocking. "If this place is lame or if anyone tries to pry out my eyeball, we're leaving pronto."

Shell nodded solemnly. "Deal."

Their heels echoed off the cracked pavement as they hurried toward what appeared to be the front entrance. Once they got within seeing distance of the tiny square window in the door, it swung open, revealing a pro wrestler–sized man in a black T-shirt.

"Card," he barked.

Shell stepped forward, holding the card out. The bouncer took it, scanned it over quickly, and then asked for IDs, which he scanned and handed back. When he held the door wider, it appeared they'd passed the popularity and age test.

Then again, both of them were pushing twenty-seven and could no longer be confused with underage drinkers anymore. Sigh. Growing old sucked sometimes.

The entrance to the club was a narrow hallway with track lighting. The walls were black. The ceiling was black. The door up ahead was black. Bridget's soul was dying a little at the lack of color and splash.

When they arrived at the second door, it too opened,

showing another big dude in . . . a black T-shirt. Bridget was starting to detect a theme here. Shell gave a little squeal as she slid past the second bouncer, giving him a long look, which was returned threefold.

Bridget's first glance around the main floor of the club was impressive. Whoever had designed this place had done well. Nothing inside gave an indication that this used to be a warehouse.

Lighting was dim, but not the shady kind of lighting that everyone looked good in at three a.m. A girl sometimes just couldn't catch a break. Several large tables surrounded a raised dance floor that would be treacherous as hell getting up and down from while drunk, but it was packed with bodies. Large, long couches lined walls painted in blood red. A spiral staircase led to the second floor but there, bouncers were blocking the top landing.

From what Bridget could see, there looked to be private alcoves up there. She bet there were a whole lot of shenanigans going on in those shadowy cubbyholes.

Behind the staircase was a sprawling bar run by eight bartenders. Never in her life had she seen so many bartenders actually working at once. Four men. Four women. All of them dressed in black, mixing drinks and chatting with the patrons.

The place was busy but not overly packed like most of the clubs in the city. And instead of stale cigarette smoke, beer, and body odor, there was a clove-like scent in the air.

This place was definitely not bad.

Shell spun toward her, clutching her black clutch in her

hand. "Tonight is going to be a night you never forget. Mark my words."

Bridget smiled.

Another shot made its way from Chad Gamble's hand to his mouth. The bite of alcohol watered his eyes, but like any family with a real good alcoholic circling around, it would take an entire keg of this shit to get him drunk.

And by the looks of those at the club tonight, getting drunk instead of laid was looking more and more like the outcome. Not one female had caught his attention. Sure, plenty of beautiful women had approached him and his friend Tony.

But Chad wasn't interested.

And Tony was more caught up in giving Chad shit than anything else. "Man, you've got to calm this crap down. You keep ending up in the papers, the Club's gonna come down on you like a ton of bricks."

Chad groaned as he leaned forward, motioning at Bartender Jim. He wasn't sure if that was his real name or not, but hell, he'd been calling the man that for about two years now and never been corrected.

"Another?" Bartender Jim asked.

Chad glanced at Tony and sighed. "Make it two shots."

The bartender chuckled as he reached down, grabbing a bottle of Grey Goose. "I have to side with Tony on this. Signing a contract with the Yankees makes you a traitor to half the world."

Chad rolled his eyes. "Or it makes me smart and incredibly career oriented?"

"It makes your agent a greedy bastard," Tony replied, thrumming his fingers off the top of the bar. "You and I both know the Nationals are paying you enough."

Bartender Jim snorted.

The Nationals were paying him more than enough—enough that by the time retirement age came around, he'd be more than set. Hell, he had more money now than he even knew what to do with, but at thirty, he had another six years left in his pitching arm, maybe more. Right now he was still in his prime. He had it all—God-given skill with a wicked fastball and precise aim; experience with the game; and, as his agent put it, a face that actually drew women to baseball games.

But the money and the contract offers rolling in weren't the problem with the Nationals.

Chad was—or his "hard partying lifestyle" or whatever the gossip column had called it. According to the *Post*, Chad had a different woman every night and while that sounded damn fun, it was far from the truth. Unfortunately, he had enough relationships that whatever was written about him was believed by the masses. His reputation was as well known as his pitching arm.

But when fans were more concerned with whom he was screwing instead of how the team was playing, it was bad news.

The Nationals wanted to keep him on, which was what Chad wanted, too. He loved this town—the team and coaches. His life was here—his brothers and the Daniels family, who had been like parents to him. Leaving the city meant saying good-bye to them, but the team demanded that he "settle down."

Settle the fuck down, like he was some kind of wild college kid. Settle down? Sure, he'd settle what he'd been told was a rather fine ass in this barstool.

Chad took the shot, slamming the glass back down. "I'm not going anywhere, Tony. You know that."

"Good to hear." Tony paused. "But what if the Nationals don't re-sign you?"

"They'll re-sign me."

Tony shook his head. "You better hope they don't get wind of what went down in that hotel room on Wednesday night."

Chad laughed. "Man, you were with me Wednesday night and you know damn well nothing went down in that hotel room."

His friend snickered. "And who's going to believe that if those three ladies say differently? And yeah, I know calling them 'ladies' is stretching it, but with your reputation, the Club will believe anything. You just need to keep a low profile."

"A low profile?" Chad snorted. "Maybe you didn't understand me. They don't want me to keep a low profile. They want me to *settle down*."

"Hell," Tony muttered. "Well, it's not like they're asking you to get married."

Chad shot him a look. "Actually, I'm pretty sure they want me to find 'a nice girl' and 'stay out of clubs' and—"

"Clubs like this one?" Tony chuckled.

"Exactly," he said. "I need to revamp my whole image, whatever the hell my image is."

Tony shrugged. "You're a player, Chad. Stop being a player."

Chad opened his mouth. Well, he really couldn't argue against that statement. Settling down was not in the Gamble brothers' vocab. His brother Chase didn't count anymore. Traitor. Chad loved his soon-to-be sister-in-law Maddie and she was great for Chase, but Chad and their other brother, Chandler, were not going to find themselves shackled to any female anytime soon.

"If you say 'don't hate the player, hate the game,' I'm going to knock you out of your seat," Tony warned.

He laughed. "You need to screw or something. Get some of that angst out of your ass. Even if I decide to go with another team, I'm not breaking up with you."

Tony flipped him off as his dark eyes scanned the floor behind them. His friend leaned back suddenly, lips pursing. "Ah, I've never seen these two before. Interesting . . ."

Chad twisted at the waist, searching down to find what had caught Tony's interest. Must be something pretty damn good because his friend was as bored with the night's offerings as he was.

His eyes scanned over a tall, slender blonde with a leather choker, dancing with a shorter woman. They were staring directly at Chad and Tony, but they were regulars. He checked out a few more women but wasn't seeing anything new. He started to turn back around when he caught sight of hair the color of dark wine.

Damn. He always had a thing for redheads.

Chad turned around fully.

The woman was standing next to a blonde who was placing a drink on one of the high tables, but his eyes went back to the redhead. She was tall—her head would probably come up to his shoulders, and he was a good six and a half feet standing straight. Her skin was like unblemished porcelain, fair and easily flushed. He couldn't tell what color her eyes were from here, but he was betting they were green or hazel. Her lips were pouty, shaped like a bow; the kind of mouth that begged to be claimed and then would haunt men's dreams long afterward.

Chad's gaze dipped and, oh hells yes, his dick, which hadn't been active all night, stirred to life. The red dress ended just below the elbows and above the knees, but he saw enough to know he liked—a lot. The material stretched across her full breasts. Chad wanted to take off the belt around her waist and use it for other things. She was rocking the kind of body pin-up models of the fifties showed off—a true woman's body. One that demanded hands and tongues trace the curves of, if they dared, and, oh yeah, he dared.

"Hot damn," Chad murmured.

Tony chuckled deeply. "The redhead, huh? Saw her first. Bet she could handle just about anything thrown her way."

Chad cut his friend a dark look. "The redhead is mine."

"Oh, simmer down, boy." Tony raised his hands in mock surrender. "I like the blonde, too."

He held Tony's gaze long enough for his friend to get that he wasn't fucking around before he turned his attention back to the redhead. She was sitting at the table now, fiddling with the straw in her drink. One of the regulars stopped by her table—Joe something or another—making a beeline for the fresh meat. Joe worked for the government, doing fuck knows what. Chad never had a problem with the guy before, but it took everything in his self-control not to get up and physically remove him.

Joe said something and the blonde laughed. The redhead flushed, and now Chad was hard as freaking granite. Man, he wanted to know if that flush traveled down and how far it went. No—he *needed* to know. His life depended on it.

"Fuck," he said, glancing at Tony. "Have I told you how much I think Joe is an asshole?"

Tony chuckled. "No, but I can guess why you think so."

Nodding absently, his eyes narrowed on the redhead. Whoever she was, she wasn't going home with Joe tonight. She was going home with *him*.

Chapter Two

The people who frequented Leather and Lace were . . . *friendly*. Already, two different men and a woman had stopped by their table, chatting casually and openly flirting. If Bridget were into girls, the flaxen-haired beauty who'd been eyeing Shell would've definitely done it for her, but the two men barely sparked any interest, which was weird, because they were good-looking and charming. One of them had showered her with a lot of attention, but she was feeling oh so very meh about it.

There was a good chance her vagina was broken or something.

Sighing, she finished off her drink while Shell practiced her seduction technique on some dark-haired guy named Bill or Will. The heady thrum of music easing out of the speakers made it difficult to hear what they were saying to each other, but the odds Bridget would be calling a cab later tonight were high.

Or worse, even using the Metro, which she was convinced was one of Dante's circles of hell.

When she got home, she'd dive into that Reese's pie she discovered in the local market earlier and that book she'd totally stolen off of Maddie's desk when she'd left work. Bridget had no idea what it was about, but the cover was green—she loved the color green—and the dude on the cover was hot. Oh, and she needed to feed Pepsi, the alley cat she'd found in a Pepsi box when he was a kitten.

Wait.

It was a Friday night, she was at a club, and a good-looking man was currently giving her the I-want-to-take-you-home-and-I-hope-I-last-longer-than-five-minutes look . . . and she was thinking about pie, a young adult book, and feeding her cat.

She was so turning into the cat lady at twenty-seven. Sweet.

"I'm heading to the bar," Bridget announced, thinking she could at least be drunk and not care how her evening turned out. "Either of you two want a refill?"

Bridget waited for a response, but after a few seconds, she rolled her eyes and stood. Picking up her mauve clutch, she slipped around the table and headed toward the bar. It had gotten fuller since they'd arrived. Squeezing in next to a woman with short, spiky black hair, she leaned against the bar.

Surprisingly, a bartender seemed to appear out of thin air. "What can I get you, sweetie?"

Sweetie? How . . . sweet. "Rum and Coke."

"Coming right up."

Bridget smiled her thanks as she glanced down the bar. Several people were paired off, a few were alone or chatting with those standing by the bar. She caught sight of a guy with dark hair and eyes and thought she'd seen him before.

A tall glass was placed in front of her and she opened her clutch, reaching for some cash.

"I have it covered," a deep and smooth voice intruded. A large hand landed on the bar beside her. "Put it on my tab."

The bartender turned to help someone else before Bridget could politely refuse. Accepting drinks from strangers was a no-go for her. Candy was a different story.

She turned halfway, her gaze following those long fingers to where a dark sweater's sleeve was rolled up to the elbow. The material clung to a thick, well-muscled upper arm, which connected to broad shoulders she found vaguely familiar. Whoever the guy was, he was exceptionally tall. Nearing six feet herself, she had to tip her head back to meet his eyes, and that made her all kinds of giddy.

Though the moment she saw his face, all giddiness vanished, replaced by about a thousand different emotions she couldn't even begin to separate. She *knew* him. Not just because everyone in the city knew who he was, but she *really* knew him.

One didn't forget a face like his or the qualities he shared with his brothers. Wide, expressive lips that looked firm and unyielding. Dominant. The curve of his jaw was strong and his cheekbones broad. His nose was slightly crooked from taking a ball in the face three years ago. Somehow the imperfection only made him sexier. Thick, coal black lashes framed eyes the color of the deepest ocean water. His dark brown hair was cropped short on the sides and longer on the top, styled in a messy spike that made him look like he'd just rolled out of bed.

Chad mother-freaking Gamble. All-star pitcher for the Nationals, middle Gamble brother, and older brother to one Chase Gamble, who just happened to be the boyfriend of her boss/coworker Madison Daniels.

Holy crapola.

She'd heard a lot about him from Madison. Part of her felt like she even knew him. Her friend had grown up with the Gamble brothers and been in love with one of them her whole life, but Bridget had never seen Chad out and about, at least not up close like this. They didn't run in the same circles, obviously. And he was here, at a club rumored to be all about sex, and he'd bought *her* a drink?

Was he confused? Drunk? Took too many balls to the face? And dear sweet Mary mother of baby Jesus, that was a fine-looking face.

Based on what Maddie had said about him and what the gossips reported in the papers, Chase was a well-known womanizer. Bridget had seen in the rags the women he was out and about with. All tall and insanely gorgeous models, and definitely not women who were entertaining thoughts of pie and paranormal books.

But he was looking at her like he knew what he was doing. Color her surprised and intrigued. "Thank you," she finally managed after staring at him for God knew how long like a total goober.

Chad's easy grin created a flutter deep in her belly. "My pleasure. I haven't noticed you before. My name is—"

"I know who you are." Bridget flushed hotly. Now she sounded like an über stalker. She considered telling him how she knew, but on a whim decided to just see where this went. There was a good chance once he knew of their six degrees of separation—aka "I might run into you again someday"—relationship, he might just offer her a wave goodbye. This player was not known for his longevity anywhere except on the field. "I mean, I know *of* you. Chad Gamble."

The grin went up a notch. "Well, you have me at a disadvantage. I don't know you."

Still flushing, she turned and picked up her drink, needing a healthy dose of liquid courage. "Bridget Rodgers."

"Bridget," he repeated, and good Lord in heaven, the way he said her name was like he *tasted* it. "I like the name."

She had no idea what to say, which was shocking. Normally the social butterfly, she was thrown for a loop. Why was he, surely a god among men, talking to her? Taking a sip, she cursed her sudden inept ability at conversation.

Chad eased in between her and an unoccupied stool behind him. Their bodies were so close that she caught the scent of spice and soap. "Is rum and Coke your favorite drink?" he asked.

Letting out a nervous breath, she nodded. "I'm a fan of it, but vodka is also a go-to drink."

"Ah, a woman after my own heart." His gaze dipped to her lips and her body warmed as tension formed deep inside her. "Well, when you finish with your rum and Coke, we'll have to share a shot of vodka."

She tucked her hair behind her ear, fighting what was probably a big, goofy smile. Though she doubted this conversation was going anywhere, she was big enough to admit she liked the attention. "That sounds like a plan."

"Good." His gaze moved back up to her eyes, meeting hers and holding for a moment. He leaned in, lowering his head. "Guess what?" he said in a conspiratorial whisper.

"What?"

"The seat behind you just opened." He winked, and damn if he didn't look good doing it. "And there's one open behind me. I think it's telling us something."

Laughing softly, she couldn't fight the smile then. "And what is that?"

"You and I should sit and chat."

Her heart was thumping in her chest in a crazy and fun sort of way, reminding her of what it had been like when she was younger and the boy she'd been crushing on talked to her at a party. But this was different. Chad was different. There was a wealth of heat in his eyes when he looked at her.

Bridget glanced over to the table where Shell was still with the guy Bridget couldn't remember was called Bill or Will. "Well then, we must listen to the cosmos."

She sat and Chad followed suit, scooting the barstool over under the guise of being able to hear her better, but she knew differently. This wasn't her first time at the rodeo when it came to meeting men at bars, but Chad was ridiculously smooth. None of what he'd said sounded cheesy. His voice dripped with cool confidence and something else she couldn't put her finger on.

Sitting so close, his knee pressed into her thigh. "So, what do you do, Bridget?"

She started to say where she worked but decided against it. The fact that she knew Maddie and Chase would definitely change things. "I work downtown as an executive assistant. I know. I know. That's a glorified term for a secretary, but I love what I do."

Chad placed an arm on the counter, toying with the neck of his beer bottle. "Hey, as long as it's something you enjoy, doesn't matter what it is."

"Do you still enjoy playing baseball?" At the weird look that crossed his face, she added, "I mean, you always hear professional players either love or hate the game after a while."

"Ah, I get what you mean. I still love the game. Politics of it, not so much, but I wouldn't change what I do. I get to play and get paid for it."

"Politics?" she asked, curious.

"The behind-the-scenes stuff," he explained, taking a swig of his beer. "Agents. Managers. Contracts. All that stuff doesn't really interest me."

Bridget nodded, wondering what he thought about the heated debate going on in the sports column lately about whether or not he'd take the New York contract. She really didn't follow baseball, only ended up reading the section during a particularly boring lunch one day. Typically, she made a beeline for the gossip page, which always had a hefty amount of info on Chad, now that she thought about it.

As she finished her drink, he peppered her with questions about her background, seeming genuinely interested in what she said. When she asked him about his schooling, she pretended she didn't know what high school and college he went to, but she knew. They were the same as Madison's.

"So, you come here often?" she asked when there was a lull in conversation. Her gaze dipped to his mouth. She was having a hard time not looking there and imagining what his lips would feel like against hers, how he tasted.

"Once a month, sometimes more or less." he explained. "My friend Tony probably comes more."

Now she knew why the dark-haired guy looked familiar. Another baseball player. "Does the entire team come here a lot?"

Chad laughed deeply. "No, most of the guys aren't into this kind of thing."

"Oh? But you are?" Yeah, she assumed some of the guys were probably married.

"Most definitely." He leaned over, placing his arm on the back of her stool. "So you're not originally from the DC area?"

"Nope, I hail from Pennsylvania."

"Pennsylvania lost a treasure."

"Ha. Ha," she said, but she was secretly flattered. Of course, she'd take that fact to the grave. "And you were doing so well before that line."

Chad chuckled. "In this case, I meant what I said, but I agree. That line was bad." His face took on the shape of someone exaggerating being deep in thought, his finger tapping his chin. "Hmm. What's a better line? How about . . ."

"No, no," she said. "Let's forget about better lines. What's your worst line? That sounds like way more fun."

"My *worst* line?" His eyes twinkled. "You're assuming I *have* a worst line, aren't you?"

Bridget gestured at the bar around her with one hand while leaning closer, settling her chin on her other hand, her arm resting on the bar in what she hoped was a seductive pose. She was a little out of practice. "Given you've admitted you hang out here a lot, why yes, I do believe you have many worse lines in you, playa playa." And then she winked. She actually winked. She sincerely hoped he wasn't going to call her out for her worst flirting moves ever because she was pretty sure she'd just emptied the vault in one shebang.

Chad laughed deep and throaty, the sound thrumming down her spine. "Well, I wouldn't want to waste my worst lines on someone as sexy as you."

Bridget couldn't help it—she snorted with laughter. "Well played, sir. Well. Played." And now she was grinning like an idiot, but at least his grin made a matching set. Man, she'd forgotten how fun it was to just get out and flirt with a smart, sexy guy.

He gave a mock bow. "I try."

Two shots of vodka arrived mysteriously. Chad laughed when she had to do the shot in two gulps.

"Cheater," he teased, eyes dancing.

Waving a hand in her face, she laughed. "I don't know how you do it. That stuff is strong."

"Years of practice."

"It's good to see that you excel at something other than baseball."

His gaze settled on her lips. "I excel at many things."

Chad motioned to the bartender for a glass of water and then slid it to her. She gave him a grateful smile and took a sip.

Like one of the women in the romance books she read, she was snared in his gaze. "You know, one more line and you win a set of steak knives."

He leaned in and it felt like there was no room. Her heart sped up as his smile turned half secretive, half playful. "Many, *many* things."

Bridget flushed, blaming the alcohol. "I think you should know, I'm impervious to bar bullshit." She wasn't, of course, as her racing heart clearly proved, but damn if she didn't care.

He reached out, brushing his knuckles along her warm cheek. She shivered. "I like the way you blush."

Bridget felt even more crimson sweep across her cheeks as she reached for her water. "Hey, I thought we agreed no more bad pickup lines." Peeking at him, she found him watching her intently. Actually, she was pretty sure he hadn't taken his eyes off her longer than a few seconds.

"Well, that's no fun." But his eyes were still crinkled with laughter. His gaze flicked to the bartender. "Another drink?"

When she nodded, she ordered something with less punch to it. They resumed talking and before Bridget knew it, she had completely lost sight of Shell as the crowd in the club thickened around the bar, obscuring the view of the tables. Chad had moved closer, his entire leg now pressed against hers. The contact made her skin tingle beneath her dress.

Glancing away, her gaze found a couple dancing nearby—if you called what they were doing dancing. It was basically sex standing up with clothes on. The woman's short denim skirt was pushed high and her leg curled along the narrow slant of the man's hips. Her partner's hand was under the frayed hem as their hips grinded together. She swallowed and turned back to her drink.

"I can't believe I'm giving you my A-game here and you're calling foul ball. I'm wounded," he said, placing a hand over his heart in mock pain.

The teasing tone brought a grin to her lips. "I can tell you have self-esteem issues."

Chad laughed, the sound deep and rumbling before slowly waning off. He leaned in, his expression growing serious for the first time that night. "Can I be honest with you, Bridget?"

She arched a brow. "Do I want you to be?"

His palm traced her wildly beating pulse, his long fingers wrapping around the nape of her neck. "I saw you before you saw me. I came to this side of the bar just to talk to you."

All coherent thought fled her. Was Chad serious? And how much had he been drinking before they met up? It wasn't that she had a low self-esteem. Bridget knew she was pretty, but she also knew her body went out of fashion several decades ago and this club was packed with super-model type chicks. The kind she saw him pictured with time and time again.

But it *was* her he was talking to, touching.

Their lips were so close that their breath mingled. The steady hum of raucous conversation and music around them faded. Maybe it was the alcohol or the fact that it was Chad Gamble. Like any woman with ovaries, she had her fair share of fantasies surrounding the playboy, but everything felt

surreal. She was hyperaware of what was happening and at the same time detached from logic.

"And just to be clear, that was not a line." Chad's head tilted to the side. "I want to kiss you."

Chapter Three

"Now?" Bridget's muscles tensed and then immediately relaxed under his skilled ministrations.

"Now."

Bridget's head was tipping back, her body relaxing into his touch, pressing toward it, yielding to it. Chad was spinning a seductive web around her, blurring reality. Her throat was dry and his fingers . . . his fingers were guiding her head back farther and an ache had started in the pit of her stomach. "I . . ."

"Just a kiss." His breath danced over her cheek, and her eyes drifted shut. Bridget's hands opened and closed uselessly in her lap.

Kissing Chad in a packed bar shouldn't turn her on as much as it did. PDA wasn't something she regularly indulged in and usually made fun of when she saw it in public, especially when it was Madison and Chase because they were all over each other constantly, but this . . . this was different and before she knew what she was doing, she said yes.

Bridget didn't feel his lips on hers like she expected.

The tip of his nose brushed over the curve of her jaw,

causing her breath to catch, and then his head dipped lower. With Bridget's head tipped back, her throat was exposed to him. Her hands clenched and then his hot mouth was against where her pulse pounded.

Bridget's entire body jerked as if he were doing something far more wicked than what was usually considered a sweet gesture. The kiss was quick, but as he started to lift his head, he nipped at her neck and then she felt his tongue sweep across her skin, soothing the sting. A moan escaped her parted lips.

"See? It was just a kiss," he said, his voice deep and husky.

Her lashes fluttered open, and Chad was staring down at her, his eyes hooded. "That . . ."

His smug smile spread as he brushed his lips over hers, feather light, making her gasp. "That was? Good?"

"Very nice," she murmured.

He chuckled, and his lips brushed hers once more. "Well, I have to do better than *nice*."

Her heart doubled its beat.

His hair brushed along the underside of her chin, soft as silk, and her fingers itched to touch them, but she didn't dare move. Chad's fingers had slipped through the mass of hair, and his hand was now cradling the back of her head.

There was a moment, so full of anticipation and the unknown, that Bridget's heart stuttered, and then his mouth was against her pulse again and her body tensed tight. His lips were warm and smooth, and she got lost in the feel of them. His tongue circled the area he'd kissed, and then he moved on, trailing tiny kisses down her neck. He nipped at the skin gently, and she jerked. He repeated the tiny scrape of teeth as he went to the hollow between her neck and shoulder, chuckling against her skin when she gasped again.

"Was that very nice?" he asked.

Breathing rapidly, she squeezed her hands into fists. "It was good."

His mouth moved against that tender spot. "You're killing me, Bridget. We have to do better than good or nice."

Chad's mouth was pushing aside the wide scoop collar, exposing more skin for his oddly tender and wholly sensual explorations. He pressed a kiss to the ridge of her collarbone, and then his free hand was suddenly on her knee, his fingers slipping up under the hem of her dress, curving along her thigh, and she thought about the couple on the dance floor, of what the man's hand was surely doing under the scrape of denim, and then she stopped thinking. She'd slipped into a world where everything was about feeling and wanting, and she uncrossed her legs.

A near animalistic sound tore from Chad's throat, and if it had been quieter in the club, people would've stopped to stare. Bridget's silent invitation must've had a powerful impact on him, because the grip on her lower thigh tightened, and when he kissed the space under her chin, she was scalded.

He lifted his head, and the look in his eyes did more than sear her. It caught her on fire. His hand found hers, lightly wrapping around her fingers. "I want you. I'm not going to even fuck around. I need you. Now."

And she needed him. Her entire body had turned to liquid heat, her very veins pumping molten lava to every part of her. Never before had she had such a quick response to a man.

She wet her lips with a quick swipe of her tongue, and the blue hue of his eyes churned. Her stomach was twisting into knots and dipping, plummeting.

Chad stood, his grip not leaving her hand but not tightening. He was giving her a chance to say no. He waited.

"Yes," Bridget said.

Bridget didn't remember most of the walk. All she knew was that he'd led her around the bar and down a narrow hallway she hadn't noticed before. She was surprised that he didn't take her up to one of the shady alcoves she'd seen in the front of the bar, which she was grateful for. God only knew the kind of action those places saw on a nightly basis. They ended up in a parking garage. She'd expected him to be driving something like a Porsche or Benz, but he had a new Jeep Liberty.

Displaying basic manners, he held the door open for her. Something she couldn't remember a guy doing recently. Just as she went to slide into the seat, he growled low in his throat and turned her around, pulled her into his chest, and devoured her with his mouth and lips and oh sweet baby Jesus his clever tongue. As quickly as it began though, he was stepping away and guiding her into the car. If she'd been having second thoughts, that kiss would have totally changed her mind.

Once inside, she texted Shell and said she was leaving, keeping the fact she wasn't alone to herself. Shell responded as expected. Her friend was already in the process of leaving with the guy she'd been talking to.

On the way to his house, they talked but the conversation

was strained with anticipation. Her heart was flipping out, and he kept one hand on her knee, his thumb continuously smoothing a circle along the fleshy part.

A few times, logic crept into her thoughts. She really wasn't the type of girl to get into one-night stands. At least she knew he wasn't a serial killer, but this was Chad freaking Gamble . . . and she was Bridget Rodgers, a good twenty-plus pounds curvier than a supermodel and barely able to keep her head afloat in the finance department, and he was the city's most talked about playboy with money falling out of his ears.

She was out of her league here.

And dear God, what kind of panties was she wearing tonight? The satin black ones or the granny panties? Since she hadn't seriously considered going home with someone, if it were the granny panties, she would die.

But then his thumb made another circle and her hormones beat at her logic. Pushing aside all the ways they didn't stack up together, she concentrated on the way her body was blossoming under his slight touch.

No more than twenty minutes later, Chad pulled into another parking garage. Bridget's heart jumped.

Shutting off the engine, Chad glanced at her and gave a small, secretive smile. "Ready?"

Torn between being more ready than she'd ever been and wanting to run, she nodded.

"Stay," he ordered, and then climbed out of the Jeep with an agility that made her envious. She watched him jog around the front of the car and then come to her side, opening the door. Extending an arm, he wiggled his fingers playfully.

Taking his hand, she let him pull her from the Jeep. Chad slipped an arm around her waist as he turned her toward the door. With his size and height, she actually felt small and petite for the first time in her life while tucked against his side.

They entered a wide and toasty hallway with hardwood floors. The doors with silver numbers were in dark cherry. It smelled like apples and spice in the hallway; the complete opposite of the mystery smell that clung to the cement floors and walls of what Bridget used to think was a decent apartment building she lived in.

When they stopped outside of 3307, Chad fished out his keys and opened the door. Stepping into the darkness, he flipped on a foyer light and quickly deactivated the alarm. Bridget hung back, her fingers tightening on her clutch.

The farther Chad moved in, the more lights came on. *Opulence* wasn't even a word she would use to describe his apartment. For starters, the thing was bigger than most houses in the city. Well over three thousand square feet, and the loft-style apartment was prime real estate.

The foyer led into a spacious kitchen, which was an experience in polished granite and stainless steel, double ovens and numerous cabinets. Did he cook? Bridget stole a look at Chad as he dropped his keys on the kitchen island under a rack of pans and pictured him in an apron . . . and nothing else.

He caught her stare, and his lips spread into an easy grin. "Would you like a tour?"

"I think if I see any more I'll get jealous," she admitted.

He chuckled. "But I want you to see more."

There was more to his words, an unsaid message that had the muscles in her belly tightening. She stepped forward and followed him out of the kitchen and into a formal dining room.

The long and narrow table surrounded by high-back chairs was minimalistic and gorgeous. Placed in the middle of the table was a black vase full of white flowers.

"I don't ever eat in here." Chad paused. "Okay, that's a lie. I did once when I convinced my brothers to join me for Christmas dinner."

She almost said his brothers' names but stopped herself. The image of him naked in the apron helped. "Did you cook for them?"

He arched a brow. "You sound like you'd be surprised if I said yes."

"You don't seem like the type to cook."

Chad made his way to an archway leading out of the dining area. "And what kind of man do I seem like, Bridget?"

The kind of man that would be hard if not impossible to forget after spending a night with, but she didn't say that. Bridget just shrugged, ignoring the knowing look that settled across his striking features.

The TV in the living room was grossly large, taking up almost an entire wall. A leather sectional couch and recliners formed a circle around a glass coffee table covered in sports magazines.

Chad pushed open a door underneath a spiral wooden staircase leading upstairs. "Here's my library, where I don't do a lot of reading but mostly play Angry Birds on the computer."

Bridget laughed, holding her clutch tightly as she peered around him. There were shelves lined with books, so she doubted the not-reading part unless they were there for pure looks. There were also several signed balls and mitts in glass cases hooked to the walls, mixed among encased autographed photos. It was like a baseball hall of fame up in here.

Easing the door shut, Chad nodded toward two doors beyond the staircase. "That leads to a guest bedroom and a bathroom. Upstairs?"

Her stomach flopped like she was sixteen again as she nodded, and they went upstairs. There was another bedroom used for guests, a room she soon dubbed the "white room" due to the walls, ceiling, bed, and carpet all being white. She was half afraid to step into that room.

But then he brushed past her, sliding a hand along her back as he headed down the hall, leaving a trail of hot chills in its wake. She could see down into the living room, but due to a nasty fear of heights, she backed around from the banister.

Chad nudged his bedroom door open with his hip and flipped a switch on the wall. Soft yellow light flowed across polished floors. A bed the size of a pool was in the middle of the room. He pulled a cell phone out of his pocket, tossing it carelessly onto the nightstand as if the phone didn't cost three months' worth of Bridget's rent.

Dressers that matched the headboard sat against the opposite wall, identical to the bed stands on either side of the bed. A TV hung from the wall across from the bed and a door opened to a walk-in closet that nearly brought Bridget to her knees.

"Your closet," she said, making her way to it. "I think it's the size of my bedroom."

"Originally, this was all one large room, but the interior designer built this closet and the bathroom."

The room was larger? Jesus. Her gaze traveled over the arms of dark suits and then polo shirts all color coordinated. On the shelves above, stacks of jeans—designer, no doubt—rested. Her closet at home was an extra bedroom and a bunch of cheap clothing racks. She could live in Chad's.

Knowing that the longer she stared into the closet, the more envious she'd become, she turned as Chad came up behind her, slipping an arm around her waist.

"I'm glad you said yes," he said, his warm breath dancing along her cheek. "Actually, I'm thrilled that you said yes."

Bridget tensed as heat swathed the length of her back. She turned her cheek toward him, biting down on her lower lip as his cheek grazed hers. The question blurted out of her mouth before she could stop it. "Why me?"

"Why you?" Chad pulled back a little and turned her around so that she faced him. He frowned. "I'm not sure I follow your question."

Her cheeks flushed as she tried to look away, but he caught the edge of her chin in a gentle grasp. Damn the absence of a filter. She cleared her throat. "Why did you want me to come home with you?"

Chad cocked his head to the side. "I think it's pretty obvious." His other hand slid to the curve of her hip, and he tugged her forward. She could feel him against her belly, hot and hard. "I can go into more detail if you want."

"I . . . I can tell, but you could have any girl at the club. Some of them—"

"I know I can have any woman there."

Well, he definitely wasn't lacking in the self-esteem department. "What I'm trying to say is that out of everyone there, you could've taken home one of the girls who looked like she stepped off a runway."

Chad frowned. "I did take home the one I wanted."

"But—"

"There isn't a 'but' in this." He cupped her cheek, tilting her head back. When he spoke, his lips brushed hers. "I want you. Bad. Right now. Against the wall. On my bed. The floor and maybe in the bathroom later. I have a shower stall and a Jacuzzi we could put to really good use. I know you'd like it."

Dear God . . .

His smile was pure sex. "It doesn't matter where. I want to fuck you in all those places." His lips swept across hers in a feather-light brush, and his voice dipped to a sinful whisper. "And I will."

Bridget's eyes widened—shocked by how much she enjoyed his vulgar language, but before she could respond, his mouth claimed hers in a deep, searing kiss that sparked a fire within. He pushed her back, fitting his hard body against hers. His hand left her cheek, drifting down her shoulder to the curve of her waist. And he kept kissing her—kissing her in a way a man had never kissed her before, as if he was drinking her in, taking long deep drafts, and her body melted against his. Bridget's hips tilted into him, and she was rewarded with a deep, throaty growl.

Lifting his head just enough that his lips left hers, he said, "Are you still confused about why I brought you home?"

"No," she breathed, dazed.

"Because I can keep showing you—actually, I want to show you." His teeth nipped at her lower lip, and her chest rose against his. "I'll admit I'm thrown off by this, too."

Second thoughts? Damn it. "You are?"

Chad nodded as both his hands landed on her hips. "Normally, I'd just get down to business. Get us off at the same time, the way we like it."

Bridget had no idea what he was talking about or how he knew the way "they liked it." All she did know was that his hands were making their way down her thighs, inching closer to the hem of her dress. Her head fell back against the wall as the tips of his fingers finally touched her bare skin.

"God, you're sexy."

Closing her eyes, her back arched, and he kissed the expanse of her bared throat as his hands slid back up her body, stopping just below her breasts. His lips found hers again, slipping his tongue inside. "I want to be inside you. All night. But I need to feel you, and then taste you first."

Chapter Four

Her eyes snapped open, protests forming on her tongue, but his hands found her heavy, aching breasts and those capable fingers swept over the material of her dress, rubbing the swollen peaks. She moaned his name then, already beyond reason, and his mouth closed over her breast, hot and demanding through the dress and the thin lace of her bra. Sharp tingles shot through her.

Chad lifted his head, covering her swollen lips with his again as he palmed her breast in one hand and finally—*finally* slipped the other under her dress. Using one powerful thigh, he parted hers and then his hand was on her inner thigh. She gasped as she felt his knuckles brush along her center.

"Damn," he groaned. "You're so wet."

She was. She was drowning for him.

One finger moved along her core, stroking her slowly. "Have you ever been this turned on before?"

Placing her hands on his broad shoulders, her fingers dug into the soft material of his sweater. Lost in the building sensations, her body arched against his torturous movements.

"Tell me," he growled.

What was he asking? When the question resurfaced, she couldn't believe she'd even consider answering, but then his fingers stopped. Bastard.

"I bet you haven't." His lips traced the heat across her cheeks, then down her throat as his fingers resumed their idle back and forth motion. "Not if you've been with men who don't know where to stick their fingers, let alone their dicks."

The fact that the way he was talking to her was actually turning her on was a bit unnerving. It wasn't like she was used to dirty talk. "You feel so good" was the extent of bed-talk she had experience with, but those crass words coming out of his mouth were making her think and want crazy, delicious things. "What about you?" she asked.

Chase chuckled against her throat. "I know exactly where to stick my fingers and my dick."

"That's good to hear."

The answering laugh sent a shudder through her. His voice sharpened. "So? Did those other men know how to use their fingers and dick?"

For crying out loud, she couldn't believe he was asking this question and she was going to answer. The words sort of tumbled off her lips, falling like drops of rain between them. "They were okay."

"Okay." Distaste clung to the single word. "Did they make you come?"

Oh, for God's sake. Her eyes snapped open and that cocky grin he was wearing infuriated her. "Are you going to?" The question was out of her mouth before she could stop herself.

The blue hue of his eyes heated. "A little demanding, are you?"

Bridget didn't respond. She really couldn't, because those agile fingers of his slipped under the satin of her panties. Her body jerked and that grin of his turned knowing. Challenge had flared in Chad's eyes, and it was obvious this man never backed down from one. Excitement pulsed in her blood like a euro techno song.

"Why won't you answer the question?" he asked. The pads of his fingers brushing against her in a way that sent another jolt through her.

Because she was having a hard time breathing. "It's a personal question."

"A personal question? Aren't we getting personal right now?"

Good point. When she didn't answer, his thumb pressed down on the bundle of nerves and she cried out, her hips arching into his hand.

"I've kissed you. Here," he said, capturing her lips in a quick, burning kiss. "And I've kissed you here." His lips moved down her throat as his other hand teased the aching peak of her breast. "And I've touched you here . . . and I'm touching you lower now."

To prove his point, one finger slipped inside her and she gripped his shoulders. "Chad . . ."

"But all of this is not too personal?" he asked, grinning as he moved his finger in and out, over and over until Bridget was breathless. "Bridget?"

How easily he'd taken over her body, astonished her, and when he cupped her intimately, still pushing his finger in and out of her, she felt the tight stirrings of release deep in her belly.

Chad seemed to know, because he picked up the pace as he tipped his head down. The soft edges of his hair brushed her cheek as he spoke into her ear. "That's okay. You don't need to answer, because whatever they made you feel is nothing in comparison to how I'm going to make you feel. And I promise you it will be more than just *okay*."

Her heartbeat skyrocketed as the sinful promise weaved its way around her. Oh yeah, Bridget was sure all of this was going to be more than okay.

Chad said nothing as his slipped another finger inside her, but he watched her—oh, his eyes were latched onto hers the whole time he worked her, refusing to allow her to look away, to escape the maddening rush of feelings he was creating.

A self-satisfied grin played across his lips as he brushed his thumb over the sensitive part of her, his eyes burning as she sucked in a shrill breath. He began tracing an idle circle around the tightened bud, coming close to touching it, but always straying away at the last moment. After a few circles, she was panting—absolutely freaking panting.

And Chad reveled in that. "I love the way you look right now."

"You do?" Her hips moved forward, but Chad pressed in, stilling her movements.

"Stay still," he ordered gruffly. His thumb made another enticingly close circle. "Your cheeks are flushed and lips swollen and parted. Beautiful."

Bridget felt like she was burning up inside, turning into a

pool of heated water. Her hands slipped down his chest, and she was awed to find his heart pounding against her palm. She ached to move into the wicked touch, but she was imprisoned between him and the wall. The evidence of his arousal now pressed against her hip heightened the yearning sweeping through her.

And when he did something truly devious with his fingers, she cried out. Her soft mewls, his slow, sensual assault, it was all driving her toward the edge. Her back arched as far as he'd allow it. She felt him grin against her flushed skin.

With his lips within kissing distance, he said, "I'm going to make you come in less than a minute."

Her breath caught. "Less than a minute?"

"Less than a motherfucking minute," Chad replied, grinning—really grinning. Not a smug one but a playful one, and her heart stuttered when it shouldn't—it couldn't, because this wasn't anything about the heart and she really didn't know him. "Yes. It will be that impressive," he added.

Cocky son of a bitch—he *really* had magic hands. Playtime was so over. His finger moved in and out, fast and then faster. In a matter of seconds, she was squirming, her breathing halting in her throat.

His lips parted. "Forty seconds to go . . ."

The next pass of his thumb created an outrageous friction. She thrust to draw him closer, deeper.

Chad growled deep in his throat. "I like that—like how your body responds to me. Perfect."

Sweet agony barreled through Bridget. Her legs stiffened. Oh, oh God . . .

"Thirty seconds . . ." he said, lowering his mouth to hers. He suckled there, matching what he was doing below with his fingers. He pulled back and murmured, "Twenty seconds . . ."

My God, he was really going to count down? He was absolutely insane.

And then he nipped and tugged on her lips as his fingers pushed in, twisting. Her body was out of control, it seemed: grinding against his hand, seeking more. Muscles coiled and tightened. Lightning raced down her spine, firing at each vertebra. Her toes curled in her boots as her hips raised clear off the wall. She gasped for air. Every single nerve ending was poised to fire.

"Come for me," he commanded.

And then his hand below moved, rolling the bundle of nerves between his fingers, and he pinched.

Release shattered through Bridget, swift and powerful, tossing her up, spiraling her in the air as sweet waves of pleasure racked her body. Thoughts scattered as she broke apart and was slowly, deliciously pieced back together.

Limp, sated, and *mind-blown*, she settled against him, gasping for air as aftershocks rippled and blew her mind a little more. She opened her eyes, finding startling blue ones staring back.

"I had five seconds left," he murmured, his hand still cupping her intimately.

Holy crap . . .

His lips tipped up on one corner. "And I still need to taste you."

Bridget slumped against the wall, her heart trying to

throw itself out of her chest. Sublimely dazed, she watched him through heavy lids.

Slowly, he pulled his hand free and stepped back. With his eyes locked onto hers, he brought his finger to his mouth and sucked off her arousal.

Bridget had never seen anyone do that. In books, yes, but not in real life. She was shocked—turned on—and completely wrapped in the sensual wickedness of the action.

Chad grinned. "I want more."

Her heart stuttered.

His hands settled on her hips, and he bent his head, kissing her deeply, and then his hands slid down, under the skirt of her dress. His fingers slipped under the band of her panties again. There was a pause and as he pulled back, his teeth caught her lower lip. And then he was moving down, taking her panties with him.

In a daze, she placed her hands on his broad shoulders as she stepped out of them. She thought he'd remove her dress next or at least her boots, but he settled on his knees, staring up at her through thick lashes. Like that, bowed before her, he looked like some kind of god come to life.

He was beautiful.

Chad inched her dress up. Only when the material was around her hips did their eyes lock. She was laid bare for him, her most intimate parts. For a brief moment, she wondered if she should feel self-conscious, but the near feral promise in his languid eyes made her hot and shivery.

As impossible as it felt, more heat flooded her and a need took root deep inside. She watched, unable to look away as he placed a kiss on her inner thigh and then the other. The stubble on his cheek pricked her skin, sending a rush through her.

Bridget had never been more captivated by anyone in her life. In that moment, she was owned and branded. She didn't understand the feeling, was too lost to really question it, but a twinge of unease blossomed in her breast. A man like Chad would be hard to forget, to move on from.

His breathing scorched her skin, and then his mouth was on her intimately and Bridget stopped thinking, capable of only feeling.

And he *feasted* on her.

Devoured her with his tongue and lips until her back bowed off the wall and her fingers delved deep into his messy hair.

She hissed through her teeth as her body rocked shamelessly against him. He worked her, licking and teasing until her head spun and she was sure her legs would give out. The tension coiled so deep, so tight, and so fast that she cried out.

"I can't take this," she said, tugging on his hair.

Chad clasped her wrists and forced them against the wall. As he was, between her thighs and her hands immobile, she couldn't stop him.

"You can take this," he said against her heated flesh.

Giving her no other option, Chad proved it. Kept at her until she came apart, screaming his name as her release tore through her, more powerful than the first. She couldn't breathe from the intensity of the pleasure, couldn't even form one coherent thought. When the shocks eased off, she was surprised she even survived it.

"That . . . that was amazing," she breathed unsteadily. "No, it was more than just amazing. There are no words."

Chad rose swiftly, cupping her cheeks. He kissed her deeply, and she moaned at the combined taste of him and her on his lips and tongue. When he pulled back, the concentrated lust in his gaze stole her breath.

"It was amazing." He kissed her again. "*You* were amazing."

She was? She hadn't done anything other than turn to complete putty in his hands . . . and mouth. Hey, at least she'd stayed on her feet. That *was* amazing.

Kissing her once more, he let go and stepped back, his movements stiff. "I need . . . a minute."

Bridget bit down on her lip, stopping the giggle that threatened to burst loose. She needed a nap and more of him—lots of him. "I'll be here."

"One minute."

On the way to the bathroom, she watched him tear off his sweater and the plain white shirt underneath. Thick muscles moved under the taut skin of his back, drawing her attention hopelessly. At the door, he stopped and turned to her.

Forget six-pack. This man was rocking an eight-pack. Good God . . .

"Don't go anywhere," he said.

Bridget didn't move, probably wasn't capable of it, until he closed the door behind him. Then she moved to the bed and sat on the edge, her knees weak and shaky. Chad had been right. They hadn't even had sex, and she'd never felt that way before. Part of her felt outrageously giddy and the other part . . . Yeah, she knew by the end of the night she was going to want to keep him.

Not good.

The water came on in the bathroom and the sound almost drowned under a sudden buzzing. She looked down and saw the screen on his phone light up. Her breath caught, and then her heart skipped a beat.

The name STELLA flashed across the screen, along with a tiny thumbnail picture of a woman everyone who shopped at Victoria's Secret recognized.

Bridget's stomach dropped.

She knew she shouldn't look at the text popping up in the preview screen. It was wrong, a violation of privacy and blah blah, but she looked because she was a girl, and immediately wished she hadn't.

N town 2night & want 2 c u & repeat last wknd.

It didn't take two brain cells to figure out what happened last weekend, even though the chit texted like a sixteen-year-old with ADHD. How old was Stella anyway? If Bridget remembered correctly, she was pushing, like, twenty-two and had been modeling since she was fifteen. Her career hit it big with the bombshell bra or something.

Before the text flickered out and was replaced by the black screen, Bridget got a good eyeful of the tiny picture of the model. Flaxen-haired and as tall as Bridget, the model probably weighed a buck ten. She was beautiful, with those lazy, smoky eyes that oozed sex appeal.

And Chad had been with *her* last weekend.

Realizing that, really understanding who he'd been with a mere seven days ago, doused her with ice water. Bridget's panties, wherever they were, would probably serve as a dress for the Russian-born model.

She glanced over her shoulder at the neatly made bed and the coal black comforter. She couldn't picture herself there now, splayed naked before Chad—before a man who brought home *supermodels*.

Super. Models.

What was she doing here? Besides having the two best orgasms of her life—truth—she was so out of her element it was embarrassing. She could barely rub two nickels together, but her thighs definitely had no problem doing so.

Bet Stella's thighs were the size of Bridget's arm.

Bridget stood and wrapped her arms around herself as her gaze narrowed on the closed bathroom door, and for some universally messed-up reason, her self-esteem hit the crapper and then kept plummeting.

Frozen at the foot of the bed, she wondered if Chad would have buyer's remorse come morning. Then he'd tell his brothers about the chick he accidentally brought home. Oh God, Chase would so recognize her name and she would die of embarrassment.

A ball of ugly emotions formed in her belly. She hadn't felt this way since she had tried to fit into the prom dress her mom had saved up for, and she'd busted the zipper after falling off a crash diet. Or when her last boyfriend—a relationship that ended well over two years ago—brought up the newest diet craze everyone would be talking about. It had been his way of letting her know she needed to drop a few pounds. What a bastard.

God, why must she think of *this* right at this moment?

She'd grown to love her body, the power of a woman with curves.

The only logical explanation, besides the fact that he'd been able to drive her home and appeared sober, was that Chad was three sheets to the wind.

Swinging around, her gaze landed on where her clutch had fallen onto the ground near the closet. Her flight or fight response kicked in the moment she heard the water turn off, and her chest spasmed.

In her head, she'd already left him. Now she only needed to follow through with action and not let the door hit her ass on the way out.

There was a real good chance Chad was going to come before he even got his pants off, which would be embarrassing to say the least.

Damn, he needed a minute—lots of minutes.

Shutting the bathroom door behind him, he turned on the cold water. Lust was swirling inside him, stringing him painfully tight. He couldn't remember the last time he'd wanted a woman as badly as he wanted to sink deep inside Bridget. Hell, she was the kind of woman he could lose himself in all night—all weekend.

Would she protest if he demanded that she stay for after-breakfast sex?

His lips twitched as he stared at his reflection. His hair was mussed from her hands and he could still feel her flesh spasming against his mouth. Her scent was everywhere and his cock twitched.

Shit.

Splashing cold water on his face, he reached for a towel and dabbed himself dry. He couldn't wait to strip that dress off her, settle between those lush thighs, and hear her scream his name again.

Chad groaned.

If he kept thinking like that, he wasn't going to last long enough to walk out of the bathroom.

After turning off the water, he swiveled around and thrust both hands through his hair. What he was doing tonight, bringing Bridget home, was exactly what the Club had warned him against, but it wasn't like the photo-hags had been hiding in the bar. And even if they were in his bedroom right now, it wouldn't stop him from taking Bridget.

Hell, an apocalypse wouldn't stop him.

But his eagerness, the need to be in her, made him feel strangely unsure of what he was doing. From what he knew of her, which was more than he knew about most of the women he'd slept with, he was intrigued. Actually, fucking *intrigued.*

Intrigue had never been in his vocabulary before, not when it came to women he just met. Sure, a few of them he was rather fond of. There were even a few friendships that had blossomed from hooking up, but he'd never been interested in what made them tick. And how could he be so damn intrigued after talking with her for a few hours over shared drinks?

Damn it, he was overthinking this, and he was still hard as a damn rock.

And he really needed to come out of the bathroom.

Rolling his eyes, he opened the bathroom door, swaggered out, and . . . came to a complete stop in his *empty* bedroom. He looked at the bed, expecting to find her snuggled there and waiting for him. Just like his bedroom, the bed was absent of one sexy-as-hell woman.

"Bridget?"

No answer.

Confused, he turned around. His bedroom was big but not so big he would lose a woman in it. If so, this would be a first.

His gaze fell on the closet. Remembering her fascination with it, he stalked toward it and pushed the door the rest of the way open. Thank God she wasn't in there, because that would wig him out a little. Stepping back, he looked down at his bed again. Her clutch was gone.

A slow-burning disbelief simmered in his veins as he prowled out of his bedroom and into the hallway. He stopped at the banister, placing his hands on it as he leaned over and stared down into his empty living room.

"You've got to be kidding me," he said, pushing off the railing.

Taking the steps two at a time, he hurried downstairs and went into the kitchen. He called her name once more, but there was no answer.

Chad stood before the empty wine rack, hands planted on his hips. He couldn't believe it, absolutely was fucking blown away. Bridget had left him—left him while he was in the *bathroom*.

Part of him demanded that he find her. She couldn't have gotten far, and she didn't have a way home. Before he knew what he was doing, he was at his front door. It was unlocked, most likely shut hastily.

As if Bridget had *run* from him.

Had he stepped out in an alternate universe where women left *him* without saying a word? Maybe he fell in the bathroom and hit his head.

But the longer he stood there, anger replaced the disbelief. He spun around and forced himself away from the door and went back upstairs. After heading to his bed, he swiped his phone. Only when his thumb brushed over the screen did he realize he didn't have Bridget's phone number. He didn't even know where she worked or lived.

Tossing the cell back to the bed, he sat down and flopped onto his back. "Shit."

Chapter Five

Bridget had always been a huge fan of Sundays. A lazy day where she pretty much stayed in her jammies, ordered out for delivery, and acted like a sloth.

And bill collectors didn't call on Sundays.

She tugged her hair up in a loose ponytail and shuffled into the narrow, short hallway. Rubbing the sleep out of her eyes, she walked into the end table beside the couch that was so in need of being reupholstered. Sharp pain shot up her leg.

"Christ on a crutch!" She hobbled to the side and knocked into the over-stacked bookcase, knocking down several books. They smacked off the floor, each one causing her to wince.

Pepsi, who'd been sprawled along the back of the couch, startled at the sound of her voice. The orangey hair rose on his back as he slid off the couch then hit the lamp on the end table as the feline shot toward the nearby recliner that had belonged to her parents. The lamp, which was heavy enough to dent the floor, tipped over.

Bridget cursed and shot forward, catching the lampshade. Dust flew into the air and crawled right up her nose.

She sneezed.

And her sneezes weren't the dainty kind that was barely a gasp. Poor Pepsi went bonkers at the nasal explosion and then darted under the coffee table. From there, two greenish-gold eyes peeked out.

Once Bridget had the lamp righted, she backed away slowly, before any more furniture attacked her. As she stood there, she couldn't help but look around her cramped living room and think of all the space in Chad's.

She cursed again.

I will not think about him or his wonderful apartment where there was actually room to walk around. And I definitely won't think of his magical mouth and tongue. The mantra had so not been working since Friday night. All day yesterday she'd avoided Shell's calls just so she wouldn't be tempted to tell her about what had happened between her and the city's beloved playboy.

But once her brain went there, it really went there. Memories of how he'd looked at her, the feel of his lips against her skin, and those fingers plagued her every step.

Stopping in front of the door, she squeezed her eyes shut and her hands into fists. Were her legs trembling? Gawd. Yes. They were. For probably what was the hundredth time in the last thirty or so hours, she told herself that she had made the right decision by bailing on Chad. Come morning, he would've surely regretted bringing her home and honestly, in those few hours, she had already started to feel way too much for him.

Way. Too. Much.

Love at first sight didn't exist but lust at first sight did, and powerful lust could quickly turn into something more. The last thing Bridget needed was a broken heart to go along with her broken wallet.

She opened the door and quickly kicked her leg out. Pepsi, as expected, bolted toward the door. When he met the pink-and-blue-plaid obstacle, he sat down and put his ears back.

"Sorry, bud—it's for the best." Bending down, she grabbed the Sunday paper just as the door across from her swung open.

Todd Newton was doing the same thing, except Bridget had a hell of a lot more clothes on than him. Dressed only in his red-and-blue-striped boxers, he did have a body made for walking around in next to nothing. Normally Bridget was all about catching a glimpse of him, but after seeing Chad's insane stomach, she barely raised a brow or felt any kind of stirring or interest.

Glancing up as he straightened, he sent Bridget a warm grin. "Hey there, Miss Rodgers."

Bridget smiled. "Morning, Todd."

His gaze dropped to where Pepsi glared at Bridget's leg. She sent him another smile as she precariously moved her leg out of the way and shut the door just as Pepsi pounced. The damn cat hit the door with an audible *thud*.

Sighing, she shook her head as she reached down and picked him up. "You're going to have brain damage along with a weight problem if you're not careful."

The cat let out a pitiful meow.

Pepsi was what Bridget liked to call plump. In reality, the cat was about the size of a wiener dog and probably outweighed one. One would think the cat wouldn't be so damn fast, but the thing was a ninja when it came to trying to escape.

Cradling Pepsi in one arm and the newspaper in the other, she headed into her small kitchen. Putting them both down on the table, she punched the coffee machine on and then opened up a can of kitty chow.

Bridget's mom would've shit a brick if she knew she let Pepsi on the kitchen table, but it wasn't like anyone other than Bridget was eating off it. Her last serious boyfriend had a huge problem with it, too.

Her ex had problems with a lot of things.

Taking her cup of coffee, which was more sugar than anything else, and the bowl of food back to the small round table, she sat down and eyed the cat. "Hungry?"

Pepsi sat back on his haunches and very slowly lifted a paw, as if to say, *Hand it over, lady, you're working for me.*

She sighed and leaned over, putting the dish in front of the feline. Sipping her coffee, she cracked open the newspaper and scanned the headlines. It was the same as it was every day—economy in the crapper, presidential candidates promising the world, and some poor soul murdered the night before. Was it any wonder she skipped to the gossips?

She really shouldn't look, especially after Friday, but her fingers had a mind of their own, flipping past the finance and sports sections.

Bridget gasped and nearly dropped her cup. With a shaky hand, she put the cup down.

Star Pitcher Gamble Goes for a Triple Play and Scores!

The headline alone was bad enough, but the picture—dear God, there was a picture?—caused an irrational surge of hot jealousy.

In true black-and-white grainy glory, in the middle of three very scantily clad women sprawled across a bed, was one Chad Gamble, grinning like he'd just hit the jackpot of half-naked chicks.

"Holy crap." Bridget grabbed the paper and lifted it closer to her face. None of the women were Stella, the model who apparently wanted a repeat of last weekend, but any one of them could easily pose for lingerie, which they were for the entire world in a bed with Chad.

A blonde had her hand on his chest. Another had her leg thrown over his. The third had her hands in his fabulously messy hair.

The article really didn't say much other than the "wild Nationals playboy strikes again." The picture was taken at a Hyatt in New York City within the pass week.

Bridget had no idea how long she stared at that picture, but the elated faces of the women blurred. Chad, well, he also looked pretty damn happy grinning from ear to ear. What man wouldn't be?

She closed her eyes and his cerulean blue eyes appeared, heated and consuming. Had he looked at those women like that? Of course he had. If she thought any differently, then she was truly an idiot. And why did she even care? She barely knew him, and it wasn't like she hadn't known his reputation.

But damn . . . that ugly feeling inside her was more than just jealousy. Possibly even a little bit of disappointment, because even though she knew that whatever had happened between them was a one-time thing, there had been moments where her imagination got the best of her. When she fantasized that he was going to show up at her door unexpectedly, having searched her out because he couldn't go on without her.

Idiot.

Thank God she didn't have sex with him and end up as another notch on a belt the size of Texas.

Bridget stood up and hurried into the kitchen. With a disgusted sigh, she tossed the newspaper into the trashcan.

God, she hated Sundays.

"Are you fucking kidding me?" Chad demanded.

From the chair beside him, Miss Stick-Up-Her-Ass shot him a nasty look. "I see language is another thing we're going to have to work on."

Chad breathed in slowly and— *Screw this*. "This is ridiculous. I don't need a babysitter."

"Miss Gore is not a babysitter," Jack Stein said plaintively. His agent had his jacket off and sleeves rolled up. Sweat beaded his brow and his dark hair looked like his fingers had made a run through them many times. "She's a publicist that the Club is requiring—"

"Requiring?" Chad planted his hands on his agent's desk and leaned in. "Since when are they requiring this?"

Jack gestured at the contract. "The Nationals are willing to re-sign you, Chad. They're willing to pay you more money—"

"But?"

Miss Gore cleared her throat. "But if you wish to continue playing for the Nationals, you will agree to get your act together . . . under my supervision."

Jack closed his eyes and blew out a long breath.

Very slowly, Chad forced himself to address her for the first time since he learned who she was and why she was there. Two dark brown eyes met his from behind square glasses. That stare made him want to cup his balls. True story.

Miss Alana Gore was the epitome of prim and fucking proper. Her dark hair was pulled back in a severe bun. Her pantsuit was a drab muddy color and ill fitting. Her shoes looked like something a nun would use to kick kids with. Not a speck of makeup covered her face. She might have actually been a decent-looking woman if she knew how to smile.

She was so not smiling right now.

Chad folded his arms. "And exactly how am I supposed to get my act together?"

"Well, for starters, try keeping your dick in your pants for longer than twenty-four hours."

Jack sounded like he choked, but Chad just stared at the woman. "Excuse me?"

Miss Gore smiled, and shit, it made her scarier. "Let me ask you a question, Mr. Gamble. Do you want to play for the Nationals?"

Stupid question. "What do you think?"

Her smile didn't fade. "And you don't want to leave the city, correct?" When he narrowed his eyes, she went on. "I've done my research on you, Chad. You have two brothers who both live in the city. You're very close with them. The three of you are all joined at the hip. No other family except the Daniels." She paused, scrunching her nose. "They run an apocalypse store?"

"It's not an apocalypse store." Chad was used to defending them. "It's a preparation store for—"

"Whatever," she said too sweetly.

Chad's skin started to itch.

"In many of your past interviews, you've stated very clearly that you don't want to leave the city or your loved ones." She leaned forward, clasping her hands around her crossed knee. "So if you want to stay here and continue to be paid to play ball, then you're going to do exactly what I say."

He turned to his agent. "This is drastic."

"Drastic?" Miss Gore bent forward and pulled the newspaper from her oversize black purse, and Chad cursed. "You were pictured in bed with *three* women."

"I didn't have sex with them!"

Both Jack and Miss Gore shared doubtful looks. "And what about the Victoria's Secret model you were seen with the weekend before?" she asked.

"I didn't sleep with her, either!" He took a deep breath. "Okay. I did sleep with her about eight months ago, but I haven't recently. We're friends."

The look on the publicist's face said she questioned his definition of friendship. "And the twins from four weeks ago?"

Good God, was this woman a stalker? "The twins *used* to date one of my brothers. We—"

"Are just friends, right?" Her smile tightened. He shot her a bland look, and she ignored him. "And then there's this club you like to frequent. Leather and Lace? Let me guess, you go there searching for new *friends*."

Chad glowered. "Funny."

Miss Gore looked rather proud of herself. The whole messed-up thing was the fact that Chad hadn't had sex with anyone in the last three months. Sure, it wasn't an astronomical dry spell, but for him, it was epic. Hell, he hadn't been interested in any woman until he stumbled across Bridget.

Shit.

That woman was the last female he wanted to think about. He was still pissed and confused about her leaving him while he was in the damn bathroom, and now he was dealing with this crap.

Miss Gore dropped the newspaper on the desk. "You probably don't know who I am, but I can assure you that nothing is more important to me than my job, and your Club hired me to repair your image."

"My image doesn't need repairing." He turned to Jack. "I didn't sleep with those women."

"Just hear her out," Jack suggested tiredly.

"It doesn't matter if you slept with an entire floor of an all girls' dorm or not," Miss Gore said. "It's all about perception, and right now the District thinks you're a whore."

Chad turned wide eyes on the woman. "Wow."

"It's the truth." She waved him off. "I have represented professional athletes, musicians, and celebrities far worse than you."

"Man, you do wonders for a man's self-esteem."

Miss Gore sat back, folding those prim hands. "Somehow I doubt you have any problems with your self-esteem. In my past experience, I have dealt with addiction, anger problems, and sexual escapades that would make yours seem like a Disney movie. Each and every one of my clients' images was beyond tarnished when I came onboard. Remember that certain child celebrity who had a penchant for cocaine and Botox injections? You don't see her at the club scenes anymore, and she's now working in Hollywood again. So I have experience with overgrown children who don't care how their actions affect other people. I have built a career on repairing images of those in the spotlight. I have never failed at it, and you'll be no different."

Oh, he was gonna be real different. "Look, I'm sure you're great at what you do, but I don't need you."

"And that's where you're sadly mistaken." Miss Gore met his stare head-on.

Chad sat down and gripped the edges of the chair. He'd never cussed at a woman before, but damn, he was coming close.

Jack cleared his throat. "I know you think you don't need this, Chad, but you don't have a choice."

"Bull. Shit."

As if he expected that kind of response, Jim opened a file and handed several papers stapled together over to Chad. He took it, quickly realizing it was his contract, and opened to the stipulations page.

He scanned it and breathed, "Shit."

"I'm sorry," Jack said, scratching his chin. "If you don't agree to work with Miss Gore and do what she says, the Nationals won't re-sign you—and could even let you out of your existing contract early."

He was absolutely dumbfounded.

"This *is* in your best interest if you want to continue to play ball here," Jack said.

Chad had no idea what to say. Anger and disbelief slammed into him with the force of a Mack truck, which ran him over and then backed up and did it again. Shit.

"I'll take your silence as acceptance," Miss Gore said. "We'll begin working together immediately."

"Really?" he grumbled.

"Really." She reached into her purse again and dropped a freaking encyclopedia-size file in his lap, causing him to grunt. "This is my contract."

"Jesus."

"And you will see that in your Nationals' contract you are required to sign this one." She leaned over and flicked the stack open to page twenty. "This is the list of new lifestyle choices."

Lifestyle choices? He wanted to laugh, but none of this was funny. His eyes darted over the list and he nearly choked. "Holy . . ." There were no words. Seriously.

No drinking in public. No late nights. No bars or clubs of questionable status. No women. He snorted at that. Women, as in plural, because he was a man-whore according to Miss Stick-Up-Her-Ass.

Well, and according to his brothers, but whatevs.

"This is laughable," he said finally, shaking his head. "I'm not a seventeen-year-old boy. I'm an adult."

"Good. I agree." She smiled again. "Now it's time for you to start acting like one. I expect you to look over everything there, because you will follow those rules. My reputation depends on it, and unlike you, I actually care how the public sees me."

He really didn't like this woman.

"You need to do this, Chad. I know how much this team means to you and this city—your brothers," Jack said, picking up a pen and offering it to him. "You need to sign this and just go with it. In a few months when things die down, it won't be this bad."

Chad stared at his agent, feeling like he'd just been betrayed. Then his gaze dropped to the two contracts in his lap. The thing was, he could say screw it and go free agent. The Yankees would grab him up in a heartbeat, but the publicist was right. Leaving this town and his brothers was the last thing he wanted. He and his brothers had a shitty childhood in their cold, sterile home. If it hadn't been for Maddie's family, God knew where any of them would be right now. Hell, it was Maddie's dad who used to come to his Little League games.

Dammit. This city had a ton of bad memories, but the good ones . . . Yeah, they outweighed the shit his father and mother dragged him and his brothers through. He needed to be close to his siblings or what he was doing now would seem like child's play. Leaving wasn't an option. Who was he kidding by even thinking he would? He just didn't think he'd end up here, with a babysitter. The Club had him by the balls.

He tipped his head back and groaned. "You're fucking kidding me."

Chapter Six

Every time Chase Gamble visited Madison at work, which was, like, every damn day since the two decided to admit their undying love for each other this past May, Bridget wanted to kick off her techno-colored pumps and crawl under her desk. Of course, she doubted her ass would fit in the space under the desk. Not that she was that big, but her desk was *that* small. After all, she was Madison's assistant, which meant she got the leftover, no-one-had-used-in-forever type of desks. She probably needed to stop bitching because she was lucky the thing had four legs and hadn't collapsed on her yet.

She'd spotted the tall, dark-haired club owner navigating his way through the cubicle farm outside their office before Madison did. A quick glance to the left and Bridget saw that Madison's nose was buried deep in quotes for the winter fund-raising gala.

The winter fund-raising gala.

Le sigh.

There was still time to try to squeeze under her desk or at least pretend she was on the phone, but before she could grab the receiver, the doors swung open and Chase's huge shoulders filled the gap. Big, door-busting shoulders—shoulders that reminded her of someone else, someone with a tongue and fingers to die for.

She really didn't need to think about that right now.

Bridget fixed a bright smile on her face. "Hey, Chase."

Over at her desk, her boss's head jerked up and her lips broke into a wide smile as she spotted her guest. "Hey," she said, standing quickly. "Is it lunchtime already?"

Chase sent Bridget a quick nod before turning his full attention on Madison. "Yes. You ready?"

Pretending to rearrange the pens on her desk, Bridget tried desperately to ignore the heavy and extremely long-lasting, PDA-filled meet-and-greet going on no more than five feet in front of her.

But Bridget looked up.

She always did, even more so now, because instead of seeing Chase and Madison, she saw Chad . . . and her. She was pathetic.

A sharp pang sliced her chest, ripping open a fresh wound that shouldn't even be there. She sucked in a quiet breath as she watched Chase kiss Madison like she was the air he needed to breathe—and that's when she looked away, blinking dry eyes.

It wasn't Chase—God, no. It wasn't Madison. Even though Bridget hadn't been a big fan of Chase in the beginning, she was happy for them. No two people were in love with each other more and they deserved happiness. Being *in* love was the key, Bridget believed with every ounce of her being. It was different than loving someone—much, much different.

But her problem was who Chase was forever going to remind her of now.

Bridget picked up a red pen that matched her cardigan and placed it in the holder that contained colored-ink pens, a black pen with the non-colorful pens. So, she might be a tiny bit obsessive over where her pens were placed.

"Bridget." Madison laughed softly. "Leave the damn pens alone and join us for lunch."

Looking up, she tucked a wayward strand of hair behind her ear. No matter how tight she pulled her hair back, the damn pieces always managed to slip through. "Oh, no, you two lovebirds enjoy your alone time."

Madison made a face as she spun and grabbed her jacket and purse. "I don't want any more alone time with him. That's why I'm inviting you."

"Thanks." Chase turned to her slowly. "My self-esteem just went through the roof."

Bridget cracked a smile at that.

"But seriously, come with us." Chase draped an arm around Madison's slim shoulders. "We're going to the new restaurant down the street."

"The Cove?" Bridget asked. Her stomach was *so* in.

"Yes." Madison grinned. "The one you've been wanting to check out. That boasts the best burgers in DC."

Chase tugged Madison against him. Any closer and the two would be sealed together. "I've ate there and their burgers are the shit."

Damn them and their knowledge of how much sway burgers held over her. Standing from her chair, Bridget grabbed her purse off the little cart beside her desk.

"Well, how can I pass up such a glowing recommendation like that?"

Chase grinned as he pivoted around. Looking over his shoulder, he said, "No jacket?"

Bridget straightened her cardigan so the embroidered flower didn't end up poised over her left breast like some kind of weird nipple. "I don't like jackets."

"She thinks they're too bulky," Madison interjected as he held the door open for them. "It can be snowing outside and she won't have a jacket on but will be wearing a scarf."

True.

Chase fell in step between them. "A scarf but no jacket?"

Bridget shrugged. "It keeps my neck warm and besides, unlike Maddie, I have a couple of extra layers worth of protection."

Her friend snorted as she shrugged on a black peacoat. "You don't have extra layers of protection, Bridget."

Confusion crossed Chase's features, and Bridget bit back a giggle. "I have no idea what you two are talking about," he said.

"Trust me," Bridget replied, grinning at Madison. "Keep it that way."

Heading down the main cluster of cubicles, she vainly ignored how her friend slowed down to an ant's crawl when they passed Robert McDowell's desk. It was common knowledge that the numbers guy had a thing for Bridget. He was nice and good-looking, but Bridget was more turned on by her polka-dotted vibrator than Robert.

And Chad—she had been really turned on by him, which

proved she had no common sense, but at least her vagina was still fully functioning.

Robert was missing a certain element. An element that even Bridget had a hard time naming, but knew it would speak to her when she saw it. Sad thing was when she met Chad at that damn club a month ago, it really had spoken to her with a bullhorn.

She'd taken two steps and Robert's head popped out from behind drab gray walls. His blond hair was a bit shaggy, framing a boyish face. "Hey there, Miss Rodgers . . ." His gaze dropped. "New shoes?"

If only she was attracted to him, Robert would be perfect. He noticed things like shoes. "Why, yes, I got them a week ago."

"Very nice," he said, sitting back. "On the way to lunch?"

She realized he might've been hamming for an invite and so did Madison, who was already opening her big mouth. "Thank you," she cut in quickly. "I'll see you when I get back."

She hurried past, feeling like one giant bitch for doing so, but she'd rather feel that way than lead the guy on or end up in an awkward moment where he inevitably asked her out and she gave some lame excuse like she was washing her cat's hair that night.

In the elevator, Madison turned narrowed eyes on Bridget. "You could've invited him, you know."

"I know." She folded her arms.

Chase leaned against the wall, tipping his head back. "Why didn't you?"

"Because—"

"Because Robert likes Bridget," Madison explained, finishing up the buttons on her jacket. "And Bridget likes pens."

"Pens?" Chase echoed.

Bridget rolled her eyes. "Pens are by far more stimulating than most people."

"I'm kind of wondering what you're doing with those pens," Chase said.

Madison scrunched up her nose. "Get your mind out of the gutter."

"My mind is always in the gutter around you."

And there they went again, inching closer and closer, arms going around each other, kissy sounds and all. Bridget closed her eyes and let out a low breath. Being around them was like standing next to two horny teenagers.

Damn, she was jealous.

The elevator couldn't move fast enough, and she was surprised Chase and Madison didn't end up having sex in the thing. A bit of the glass walls were fogged up, though.

Brisk November wind cooled Bridget's cheeks as they dodged businessmen carrying briefcases and tourists with fanny packs. Off in the distance, the Washington Monument rose like one giant . . . phallic symbol.

Men and their architectural toys . . .

Weird looks were sent their way, ones that either Madison or Chase ignored or didn't see, but Bridget saw every one of them. A red cardigan typically didn't go well with a pink-and-white-striped skirt and colorful heels and white tights, but Bridget's oddball fashion sense wasn't anything new. More like a reject from the eighties to be exact, but she'd always been this way, throwing clothes together, mix-matching designs like a trendy Euro-trash designer.

Her mother believed it was some kind of psychological misdirection enabling Bridget to protect herself from getting hurt. Eye. Roll. She just liked colors and really wished her mother were in any career, even stripping, instead of psychology.

Nothing beats getting diagnosed over Thanksgiving dinner.

Halfway there, Chase dug out his cell and chuckled, drawing both their attentions. He texted something back and then bent down, brushing his lips across Maddie's forehead.

Two blocks down from the Mall, they dipped into the trendy new diner. Warm air greeted them, as did the faint smell of grease and pricey food. The place was crowded, which made squeezing between the round tables tricky.

"Are we going to get a seat?" Bridget asked, hoping the blister she was getting on the back of her foot wasn't in vain.

Chase nodded. "I called ahead. We got a booth out back."

A frown puckered Madison's face. "I thought this place didn't do reservations?"

He smiled.

Of course, Bridget realized, no establishment in town would refuse Chase or any of the Gamble brothers. Besides the politicians and drug dealers, the Gamble brothers ran this town.

The roomy booth in the back, caddy corner to a not so surprisingly busy bar, was big enough to seat six comfortably. Madison and Chase took up one side while Bridget slid into the opposite seat, thankful she loathed jackets as she watched Madison mutter under her breath, stand again, and then take off her jacket. A server swung by their table, dropping off plastic-covered menus and taking their drink orders.

"Can I get another water?" Chase asked, spreading an arm along the back of the booth. "We have one more person joining us."

"Sure," the waitress replied, smiling.

"We do?" Madison asked once the waitress dashed away to fill the order.

The strangest feeling washed over Bridget. Kind of felt like someone had poked her in the stomach a couple of times as she stared at Chase, praying to every God she knew that he wasn't going to say what she was fearing.

Chase flipped the menu over. "Yeah, it's a good thing Richard—"

"Robert," Madison corrected.

"Didn't get invited, because Chad texted me on the way here. He's just a block down, and he's going to grab something to eat with us."

Bridget stopped breathing. And then she lost her appetite, just like that. Vanished, replaced by knots twisted more times than a Celtic loop.

Oh no, no no no . . . this could not be happening.

When she had dashed out of Chad's luxurious apartment, sans panties, she figured that would be the last she'd see of him in person. They really didn't run in the same circles, and she had sworn off sexy bars in her future.

She felt sick.

"Great," Madison said, leaning back against the seat.

"Let's see how long he goes before he gets his picture taken or asked for an autograph."

The smile that crossed Chase's face was full of pride. "Hey, he's the star. Recognize."

Bridget stopped listening to them as she glanced back through the restaurant and eyed the door. She couldn't be here. No way was she eating lunch with Chad. Panic blossomed in her belly and crawled up her throat. Good God, she hadn't even told Shell about what happened, much less Maddie.

There was a good chance she was going to hurl.

What if he recognized her?

What if he *didn't* recognize her?

She didn't know which would be worse.

"Bridget, are you okay?" Concern radiated from Madison's voice.

Nodding absently, she grabbed her purse. "Yeah, but I just remembered I had this phone call at the office. I . . . I better get back."

Madison frowned. "What phone call?"

Uh, yeah, what phone call? "I need to check in with the catering company about desserts for the gala event."

Madison's eyes narrowed. "I thought we were waiting to hear back from them."

Bridget started to stand. "Oh, yeah, but I wanted to call them—" She cut herself off. Her boss was giving her a look that said, *Sit down and stop acting weird*, and really, bolting on lunch would just look crazy.

"Never mind," Bridget said, fixing a smile on her face. "It can wait."

Madison stared at her a moment longer and then went back to chatting up Chase.

Life could be so unbelievably cruel.

For the last month, she had wrestled with what she had done and didn't do with Chad. Part of her was glad she had left before the man wised up and regretted bringing her home, but the other part, the one that operated purely on memories, rehashed the way he'd kissed and touched her over and over again. For a straight month she replayed it, unable to shake the feelings he had awakened in her and wishing she had more memories to linger over.

God, she couldn't even think about this right now.

When the drinks arrived, she swallowed a gulp, wishing there were some vodka in her diet soda. She needed to try to leave again. Had to. "Madison, I forgot—"

A low rumble from the front of the restaurant cut off Bridget and any hope she had of making a clean getaway. She didn't have to look to know that he was there. All the commotion was for him. Ball players were like gods in their hometowns.

She dropped her hands to her lap and continued staring at the menu, but when Chase greeted his brother, she had no control over herself. Not looking was like going against nature.

Worn jeans hung low from a tapered waist and the long-sleeved shirt he wore stretched taut over a stomach she knew you could do a nation's worth of laundry on. Like the other two Gamble brothers, he had shoulders a girl could hold on to. Shoulders that could bear the brunt of anything you threw his way. He had a body that was meant for sex.

She really shouldn't think of sex right now.

His attention was on whatever Chase was saying, and she was sure he hadn't even noticed her yet. Why would he when the waitress suddenly appeared out of freaking nowhere, popping a hand on a nonexistent hip as she stared up at him like he was on the appetizer menu. Bridget couldn't blame her. His easy grin made *her* stomach flutter as he took the menu from the waitress, his long fingers brushing hers as he did so.

"There's a water for you," the waitress said, her cheeks flushed and eyes bright. "Would you like something else?"

Chad shook his head. "Nope, that's perfect. Thank you."

Bridget bit down on her lower lip at the sound of his deep, smooth voice and told herself to look away, but now she couldn't. She stared at him like she was nine kinds of crazy, part of her willing him to look away and another part hoping he disappeared.

"Are you sure?" the waitress asked, batting lashes like she was having a seizure. "I'll be more than happy to get you something a bit tastier."

Madison choked on her drink.

"Water is fine, but thank you," Chad said, polite as ever. And then he added, "But I'll keep your offer in mind."

Bridget sighed, totally foreseeing an exchange of numbers in their future.

Finally, the waitress disappeared with a promise to be back to get their orders and an extra swing in her hips.

"Can't take you anywhere," Chase said, grinning.

Chad chuckled. "Whatever."

And then he reached toward Madison, no doubt about to

ruffle her hair, but she jerked back, eyes narrowed. "Do that and you won't be making the waitress's dreams come true anytime soon."

Her threat was no deterrent, though, and he managed to mess up her hair before Chase stepped in, threatening to do bodily harm.

Bridget was slowly sinking into the cushion, keeping her hands still tightly clasped. Maybe he would never notice her. Seemed probable, since he hadn't looked in her direction once, but then Chase had to open his mouth.

"Oh, you haven't met Bridget, have you?" Chase nodded in her direction, and she felt her eyes go saucer-size wide. "She works with Madison."

Oh God, oh God, oh God . . .

As if time came to a crawl and she was stuck in one of those cheesy movies, Chad turned toward her slowly. A wide, welcoming smile split his lips as his gaze flickered over her. He was already leaning down and extending a hand toward her.

Their eyes met.

The smile on his face faded as he jerked back, his eyes widening slightly in recognition.

Oh, crap.

Chad stared at her so long heat infused her cheeks, and then he spoke one word, breathed it really. "*You.*"

Chapter Seven

Holy shit, it was *her*.

Here, with his brother and Maddie. He almost couldn't believe it. He was still pretty pissed that she had bolted on him that weekend, but he'd finally come to accept that it was unlikely he'd see her again. But here she was, a month later, popping up in a restaurant in the middle of the day with *his* brother, which meant there was no way in hell Bridget hadn't known who he was related to when they met that night. First off, he looked just like his brother and secondly, everyone knew the Gamble brothers. *Everyone.*

Chad was struck stupid.

Today had started off like any other off-season day. Four-hour workout in the morning—it was true. Players really were made in the off-season—the training, the workouts. Then he managed to evade his babysitter for the rest of the morning. The stick was even farther up her ass than normal since he'd gotten caught leaving his brother's bar with Tony. Yeah, he'd been a little intoxicated, but damn, he hadn't been with a female and he'd behaved himself. Mostly. According to Miss Gore, having a few drinks was tantamount to punt-kicking a baby.

He'd kept a low profile the last month, but Miss Gore

wasn't impressed, and every time he stepped out of his house, she was right on his ass. So when Chase had texted him about lunch, Chad jumped at the chance to get out and also piss off Miss Gore at the same time. But the last thing he expected was to see *her* again.

God. Damn.

She looked just like he remembered but better. Rich auburn hair pulled back in a low bun, but he knew it was long and full of soft waves that would tumble around her heart-shaped face. Her normally porcelain complexion was flushed now and full, pouty lips parted.

Chase cleared his throat. "Uh, you two know each other?"

He couldn't stop staring at Bridget.

Her light green eyes were wide as she stared back, no doubt remembering just how well the two of them knew each other. Not as well as Chad had wanted but pretty damn close. Since she was sitting down, he couldn't get an eyeful of those lush curves. He wanted to peel off that fucking cardigan because it was way too concealing.

Bridget swallowed, and her gaze swung toward his brother and Maddie. "Um, we met briefly," she said.

Met briefly?

Maddie's mouth dropped open. "How come you never mentioned you met Chad?"

Yeah. How come? He was very, very curious and a bit offended. Why wouldn't she mention that she knew him? Then again, considering *where* they met, most people didn't bring up that club in common conversation.

Sitting down beside her, he leaned back and folded his arms. And waited.

Bridget glanced at him nervously. "It wasn't a big deal."

He was pretty confident that he was a big deal.

"And I actually kind of forgot about it." She laughed, toying with the paper her straw had come wrapped in.

She forgot about it that quickly? Bull. Shit. His ego more than a little bruised, he was about two seconds from explaining just how well they knew each other but stopped. She didn't want anyone to know what happened and he could respect that, but she was definitely going to have to re-evaluate her "not a big deal" statement later.

Going along with this, Chad smiled and decided two could play at this game. "It was a while ago—at a game or something? You asked for my autograph, I think."

Bridget's delicate brows slammed down. "No. It wasn't at a game, and I didn't ask for your autograph."

"You sure?" He glanced at his brother, who was watching them with raised brows. "Hell, I remember the face, but you're going to have to refresh my memory about the rest."

"No reason to. Like I said, it was just a brief meeting." She squirmed a little, and it drew his attention downward. The curve of her hip and thigh made his cock swell. "I'm sure there are a lot of faces you don't remember," she added.

He tilted his head to the side, not missing the sly jab. "I imagine the same could be said about you."

Her head jerked toward him, eyes a more vibrant shade of bottle green. She was angry. Good. He wasn't feeling too cuddly, either.

Across the table, Maddie watched with rabid fascination. "Okay, so where did you two meet if it wasn't at a game?"

"Good question," Chad murmured, eagerly awaiting Bridget's response.

She squirmed even more, so much so that her thigh brushed his.

"You're fidgeting," he pointed out. "And we're waiting."

"I'm not fidgeting."

He clamped a hand down on her thigh, just above the knee, and she nearly jumped out of the booth. "You're fidgeting."

Her gaze dropped to his hand, and her flush deepened. He felt her shiver, and a near feral urge seized hold of him. Instinct demanded that he keep his hand right where it was or inch it down a few centimeters and then slide it up that skirt. Speaking of the skirt, it reminded him of a candy cane. He wanted to lick those stripes, but he doubted his brother and Maddie would be interested in that kind of show.

Smiling at her, he slowly lifted his hand, one finger at a time.

His brother and Maddie exchanged long looks. Lucky for Bridget, the waitress arrived to take their orders. Everyone ordered burgers and the waitress lingered longer than necessary, which normally wouldn't have bothered Chad, but his attention was elsewhere, currently on the little liar sitting next to him.

"So, where did we meet?" he asked, grinning when she stiffened. If she thought she was off the hook that easily, she had another think coming. After a month of wondering what the hell happened to her, he wouldn't let her get away this time.

Bridget looked up, her chin jutting out stubbornly. "It was at some bar. You were there with a friend."

"Hmm, I can't recall this bar."

She shot him a glare, and Chad's grin spread. Understanding quickly flared in her eyes, and then she looked away. "Anyway, Madison almost has the numbers finished for the winter gala."

Maddie blinked. "Oh, yeah, with all the donations expected, we're hoping to raise quite a bit of money this year for the Extended Learning program at the Smithsonian."

"That's my girl." Chase bent his head, kissing her cheek.

Damn, his brother was whipped.

Sometimes it was strange seeing those two like that, especially Chase. They were perfect together, but Chad could never see himself in his younger brother's shoes, loving someone so much you let go of the past and turned your whole world upside down for her.

"We only have a month to get everything ready," Bridget chattered on, "but we've sold out the tickets."

"That's good news," Chase said. "Are you guys going to have everything ready by then?"

Maddie nodded. "Yeah, the only thing that will be last-minute will be Bridget."

Chad's interest piqued. "Why is that?"

Beside him, Bridget went stock-still as she glared at Maddie, which was blatantly ignored. "Bridget always waits till the last moment to bring a date."

"Does she?" Extending an arm along the back of their booth, he spread his legs, taking up as much room as humanly possible.

She scooted over a little, which planted her against the art deco wall. "I like to keep my options open."

For some reason hearing that got under his skin. Was that why she had disappeared? Did she see someone at the club who was a better option? Doubtful.

"Anyway," Chase said. "Back to you two. So you met at a bar and . . . ?"

Bridget's shoulders slumped.

Taking pity on her even though she didn't deserve it, he said, "You know, I think I remember now. We talked about baseball."

"Uh huh," Chase said, sounding doubtful.

Maddie looked just as disbelieving. "You talked about baseball, Bridget? You don't know anything about baseball."

"Yes. I do," Bridget huffed.

"Like what?" Maddie challenged.

Those lush lips he'd had so many plans for that night thinned. "People throw balls and try to hit them with a bat and get paid way too much for doing so. What more do you need to know than that?"

Chad tipped his head back and laughed. He had forgotten how feisty her mouth was. It hadn't been the first thing that had drawn him to her—that had been that round ass—but it definitely had hooked him in, provoking his need to control and dominate.

"Sounds about right," Chad agreed. He glanced at his brother. "I think Chase has said that a time or two."

His brother nodded.

The food arrived and for a while the topic was dropped. Everyone dug in . . . everyone except Bridget, who spent more time breaking her burger up into tiny pieces than she did eating it.

He leaned over, close enough to catch the scent of her shampoo. Jasmine. It was just like he remembered. No heavy perfumes, just the soft, musky scent of jasmine. Damn, he hadn't been able to get this woman out of his head. "Do you always play with your food?"

Bridget's head snapped in his direction and as close as he was, her cheek grazed his. She gasped and then jerked back. "I'm not playing with my food."

Chad knew he should move back, because he was far beyond the boundaries of personal space, but he didn't. Some would say he was being a bastard like that, but for him, it was fun and he liked to tease.

All different kinds of ways.

"I'm actually waiting for you to start making a smiley face out of the bun," he said.

"I could make one on your face if you wanted?" she replied sweetly.

He leaned back, chuckling. "I don't think I could let you. I've been told I have a million-dollar face."

His brother groaned. "You're never going to let the whole *People*'s Sexiest Men bullshit go, are you?"

"Never," Chad replied gamely.

"Wasn't that last year, anyway?" Bridget threw in.

Maddie giggled. "Yeah, it was."

"But this year hasn't been released yet, so there's always time." Chad winked at Bridget.

She rolled her eyes.

He nudged her arm hard enough to make her drop her fork on her plate. "I bet you'll buy that copy. Probably more than one copy, too."

She stared at him. "Your ego is astonishing."

Taking back the distance between them, he whispered for only her to hear, "That's not the only thing that's astonishing, but you already know that."

"Okay." Maddie drew out the word, looking at Chase like she expected some kind of explanation, but his brother just shrugged.

A patron of the restaurant stopped by their table, towing along a young boy wearing a Nationals ball cap. Chad was surprised to see the kid, since he was at the age where he should've been in school.

"I'm sorry to interrupt, but we're huge fans." The father clapped a hand down on his son's skinny shoulder. "Steven would love if you signed his cap."

Some of the players would be bothered by these kinds of things or charge a fee for it, but Chad thought they were giant douches. Smiling, he nodded. "Sure. I don't have anything to sign with, though."

The waitress appeared out of nowhere, presenting a permanent marker. "I'm a huge fan, too," she whispered, winking.

He bet she was a different kind of fan.

Taking the marker, he waited for the boy to remove the cap. The boy hesitated and when he finally did, Chad saw why the kid wasn't in school. Silence fell over the table. The pretty waitress cast her eyes to the ground as Steven inched closer to the table. His head was completely bald and pale white, obviously a side effect of chemotherapy.

Shit.

Signing a ball cap wasn't enough, but he flipped the cap

over and scrawled his name along the back. While he tried to write a decent signature, he sensed Bridget lean forward and he looked up.

"You're a fan of Batman?" she asked, gesturing at his shirt with her hand.

Steven nodded tentatively.

Bridget smiled, and oh, hell, there was something about that smile—something that he'd forgotten or been too horny when they'd met at the club to notice, but it was breathtaking. Lighting up her jade-colored eyes and placing two dimples in her cheeks.

She was beautiful.

"Batman is my favorite, too," she said. "He's way cooler than Superman."

The little boy warmed up, grinning a little. "Batman can't fly, but he has better weapons."

"He does!" she exclaimed, eyes dancing. "Comic? Movie?"

"Movie," the boy answered.

"Oh, I don't know about that." Bridget looked somber. "The comic is way better."

"No way!"

During the exchange, Chad watched her in awe. No one at the table, including him, had known what to say or do. Fuck, the waitress was *still* staring at the floor like it held the cure for cancer, but Bridget had jumped right in, setting the boy at ease. He also wondered if she really did read comics. Intriguing. Wait. There was that damn word again. Stopping himself right there, he didn't find it intriguing. Yeah, he was attracted to her on a near-animalistic level. Had been when he first met her and had wanted her—still did—but that was as far as he went with women. Settling down or being *intrigued* was what his team wanted for him, not what Chad wanted.

Handing the cap back to the boy, Chad smiled. "There you go, kiddo."

"T-Thank you, Mr. Gamble." Steven placed the cap back on, pulling it down low.

"No problem. I hope to see you at a game in the spring."

"You betcha," Steven said, tugging on his father's hand. "Can we? Please?"

"First game of the season," he replied, shooting Chad a grateful smile before ushering the boy off and back to the table.

In his absence, the waitress placed the checks on the table. When the receipts came, as expected, there was a telephone number on Chad's slip of paper.

Bridget saw it and smirked.

Chad's eyes narrowed.

As the four of them headed out of the restaurant, Chad discreetly tossed his receipt in the trash.

Heavy, thick clouds had moved in, no doubt bringing cold, bitter rain. Damn, he hated November. Give him snow or give him sun.

"We still on for tonight?" Chase asked, swinging an arm around Maddie.

Wednesday night was poker night. Chad kept his gaze on Bridget, who was trying to very unsuccessfully disappear behind the couple. "I'll be there at seven."

Maddie broke free and gave Chad a quick hug. "Don't be a stranger, rock star."

He squeezed her back and then patted her on the head, knowing how much she hated that. "See you later, midget."

Through the good-byes, he hadn't taken his eyes off Bridget. She was inching away, a bright and false smile plastered on her face as she clasped the handle of her purse in front of her like some kind of shield.

When Chase and Maddie turned to head back toward the Mall, Chad slipped up behind Bridget, wrapping his hand around her arm in a gentle but firm grip. She stopped, and her eyes shot wide. Before she could open her mouth, Chad cut in.

"Hey Maddie, I'm going to keep your friend for a few minutes, okay?"

Maddie looked over her shoulder, brows furrowing. "I don't know if I want to leave her with you."

Taking that good-naturedly, he grinned. "I promise I'll return her just as she was."

She glanced at Bridget, who gave a resigned sigh and nodded. Maddie smiled—the kind of smile that Chad knew all too well. Poor Bridget was going to have a field day when she got back to the office.

"Take your time," Maddie called, and then turned back around, looping her arm through Chase's.

Chad watched them stroll down the ever-busy Constitution Avenue. "They make such a cute couple, don't they?"

Bridget stepped back under the awning of a closed arts dealer shop, and he followed, keeping his hand on her arm. She blinked several times, those crazy-long lashes fanning her flushed cheeks. Damn. He'd remembered her because he couldn't forget her, but his memories hadn't done her justice.

She drew in a deep breath. "Look, I really need to get—"

Lowering his head so their faces were mere inches apart, he enjoyed the soft intake of breath. "Did you really think you were going to escape me twice, Bridget?"

Chapter Eight

Never in her life had she suffered through a more awkward lunch, and there was no end in sight. Did she plan on escaping Chad again? Well, yes. Was it working?

Her gaze dropped to where his large hand practically swallowed her arm. She could feel the heat rolling off his powerfully coiled body as if she were basking in the sun instead of standing in the chilly wind.

Nope. Her plans for escape sure weren't working.

"Bridget?"

She raised her eyes, meeting the deep blue hue of his. The feral, possessive look in his stare made her hot and shivery. Having seen that look in his eyes before, she wetted her lips. "So, you remember me?"

"Remember you?" he repeated, brows lowering. God, he was good-looking. As much as she hated to think it, there was no doubt in her mind he would end up on *People*'s list again this year. "How could I forget you?"

Her heart tripped over itself and her mouth dried. "Then why did you act like you didn't know who I was?" she accused.

"Why did you say we only met briefly and it wasn't a big deal?"

Bridget bristled. "It wasn't like I was going to say, 'Oh, I met him at a club rumored to be a *sex club.*' That's kind of private, you know. Anyway, I'm sure there are a lot of women you've met at that club, so why would I think I would've stuck out to you?"

Letting go of her arm but not moving away, he placed a hand against the brick wall beside her head. She wondered what they looked like to people passing by. It would only be a matter of time before someone recognized him.

"There's only one person who made a daring escape before the real fun got started."

She flushed. Real fun? Dear God . . .

He cocked his head to the side, eyes narrowing. "For a month, I've been dying to know why you ran." He paused, waiting. "Don't you remember the details?"

She closed her eyes. No matter how hard she tried, the details of that night had refused to be forgotten. To this day, she couldn't fathom how someone like him, a freaking god among men, would've been interested in her or even cared to know why she'd left.

"I'm more than happy to remind you," Chad offered. "You left while I was in the bathroom. I came out and you were gone. No note. No good-bye. Nothing."

"I—"

"And if I remember correctly," he said, his voice lowering to a low, sexy whisper, "I made you come twice before you ran off, so it wasn't like you weren't enjoying yourself and then some."

Oh God, her body went hot, but not because of embarrassment. The heat was from the memories his words provoked. The man's fingers weren't just skilled at handling a baseball, and his mouth . . .

Bridget shuddered.

"So, I'll ask again. Why did you leave?"

Why had she left like the very devil was snapping at her heels? It wasn't the dark, sensual promise in his cerulean eyes. Or what he had said to her. It was the wakeup call that came in the form of a text message from an incredibly beautiful Russian supermodel.

Bridget had long since accepted that she'd never be one of those women who could ever be considered petite. And normally her confidence didn't waver, but Chad had to be the kind of man who was used to tight and trim bodies. And when she saw the gossip section that following Sunday and a picture of him and those three women, she knew hightailing her behind out of there had been the right decision. Maybe Chad had been in the mood for something different that weekend, and the last thing she wanted to be was his experiment with buxom girls.

Looking away, she took a deep breath as a series of speeding taxis blew their horns. "Okay, maybe I shouldn't have left without saying something," she admitted. "But I've never done that before."

"What? Had an earth-shattering orgasm?"

Geez, that was partly true, but damn, his arrogance knew no limit. She shook her head. "No. I never went home with a guy—"

"One-night stand?" he interrupted. Doubt clouding his tone. "You've never had a one-night stand?"

Bridget looked at him. She couldn't help but be aware of how close their lips were. "It's none of your business."

"I'm about to make it my business," he replied.

She couldn't believe she was standing there with him, arguing over her sexual history. Stepping to the side, she said, "I have to get back to work. It was nice—"

Chad placed his free hand on the other side of her head, caging her in. She doubted she'd be able to slip under his arms. The look in his eyes said he might like it if she tried.

"I want to know why you ran," he demanded again.

Frustration boiled over. Her chin jerked up in defiance. "Maybe I didn't like the way you were ordering me around, telling me when to come and all."

"You were enjoying what I was doing. Don't even deny it." Chad's lips spread in a half grin. "I like to be dominant, Bridget. That shouldn't come as a shock, given where we met."

She couldn't believe they were having this conversation on the side of the street, all out in the open and stuff.

"People who go to that bar . . . they know what kind of people frequent the place." Chad paused. "Shit. You really have no idea what Leather and Lace is?"

Heat crept across her cheeks. "It's just a bar . . ."

"No. It's a bar that caters to swingers, doms, and subs."

Oh, dear God. Bridget stared at him. Up until that moment, she really hadn't believed any of the rumors, and while that was some freaky stuff right there, it wasn't why she'd bolted. She'd jump in front of a speeding taxi before she admitted why she really ran. "I was at *that* kind of club?"

He nodded.

"*You* were at that kind of club?" Holy crap, she was having images of him tying her down—she threw the brakes on that train before it could fully take off.

A smirk played across his lips. "I'm not really big in the lifestyle, but I do like to dominate in bed."

That train totally just zoomed off, throwing out silk ties and blindfolds and candle wax. All sorts of stuff she'd read in erotica.

"Okay, now that I know you had no idea what you were getting yourself into, which is sort of cute, by the way, that still doesn't tell me anything. It wasn't like I handcuffed you to the bed or scared you off."

Handcuffs? Crimmey. A low heat started in her belly, even though she wondered if she should be so turned on by the idea.

"And you had nothing to fear from me," Chad continued in a low, smooth voice. "Your pleasure would've come first every single time."

God, she wished he hadn't said that. "It doesn't matter. I'm not interested—"

"Bull. Shit. You were interested. And you're interested *now*." Chad leaned in so close that when he spoke his lips grazed her cheek, sending shivers straight to her core. "You may not have known what Leather and Lace was, but you went home with me because you wanted me. I have no idea why you ran, but still, you are *very* interested."

"I'm not—"

He swore under his breath, and then he cupped her cheeks. His hands were rough from years of playing baseball, but she liked the feel of them. He tilted her head back and with no other warning, he brought his mouth to hers, kissing away her protests and denials. His tongue swept past her lips, tangling with hers.

The kiss was one of pure dominance and control. His way of proving to her she was attracted to him and still very much interested. And there was no sense in lying or throwing up false protests at this point. Her body yielded to the kiss. Gripping the front of his sweater, she sunk into his hard body and kissed him back with fervor.

It seemed like forever before he lifted his head, breathing just as heavily as she was. Staring down at her, he swallowed hard and slowly removed his hands from her cheeks. "Like I said, you're still very, *very* interested."

Bridget didn't remember walking back to the Smithsonian. Her legs felt like jelly, and she was in a daze. Had Chad kissed her just to prove she wanted him? If so, he'd gotten what he wanted, because the moment his lips touched hers she had turned to goo.

And then he had left her, turned around and left her on the side of the street.

Not like she didn't sort of deserve it, considering she had left him without a backward glance last time.

Never in a million years would she have thought she'd ever run into Chad and be kissed by him again.

Once she shut the office door behind her, she turned and found Maddie at her desk, hands cupping her chin.

"Bridget?"

She sighed. "Madison?"

Her friend tilted her head to the side as she tapped long, manicured fingers off her cheek. "So, you and Chad . . . ?"

Shuffling to her desk, she plopped down in her seat and toed her way toward the cart. She dropped her purse on it before she answered. "What about it?"

Silence.

Bridget dared a peek at her boss. "What?"

"You two met at a bar?"

At least that part was true. Bridget nodded.

"And you didn't think to tell me?" Maddie's eyes narrowed. "It's not like you wouldn't know *who* he was or *who* he was related to."

"It really wasn't a big deal," she said, glaring at the mass of pens in their holder. Someone had placed a black pen in with the colored ones. Bastard. "I honestly forgot about it."

Madison snorted. "I don't believe you."

Snatching the black pen, she placed it with the blue ones. "We just talked. It was nothing."

"Nothing . . . Yeah, okay." Maddie sat up, crossing her arms, giving Bridget her best bullshit-detector stare. "I've known Chad my whole life."

"I know." She mirrored her friend's posture, except the stupid flower poked her in the breast.

Madison smiled a little too brightly. "Chad has always been the . . . outgoing one. Usually up to no good, but very . . . playful. When he was younger, he used to always play pranks, and even now he's really friendly."

Ah, yes, Chad was *really* friendly. Bridget schooled her expression.

The look on Madison's face said she wasn't fooled. "But I've never seen him act like he did with you today."

Bridget struggled to keep her face impassive while internally she was as curious as Pepsi strung out on catnip. "What do you mean?"

"Well, like I said, Chad has always been a friendly person, but he was so in your personal space I was pretty sure he was going to shove his tongue down your throat at some point."

Her face flushed.

Madison's eyes narrowed. "And did he grab your thigh at some point?"

"Uh, I . . . I think so." She cleared her throat as she swiveled back to her desk. Pens. Pens needed places for order. "He doesn't normally do that?"

"Only with women he's slept with," she quipped.

Bridget dropped three red pens on the floor.

"Did you sleep with Chad?" Madison asked.

The question hung in the room like a plume of poisonous gas. Bending down, she gathered up the pens and faced her friend once more. "No. I did not sleep with Chad."

Madison stared at her a long, hard moment and then said, "I believe *that* part of the story."

"*Maddie*," she said, using the nickname Chase favored.

"Whatever. Don't Maddie me. I feel offended. I know you're not being honest with me. Something obviously happened between you two." Her pout was brief, and then she stood. "You do realize Chase will probably get the truth out of him, right?"

Damn.

Her friend's eyes lit up as she moved to the front of her nice big desk and propped a slim hip against it. "And if I find out there was an exchange of bodily fluids—any type of fluid—I'm going to tell Robert that you're madly in love with him."

"That's so wrong!"

Madison shrugged.

Picking up a stack of Post-it notes, she chucked them at Madison. They missed her by a mile. Hell. There was little to no chance she was going to get out of this situation without Madison and Chase knowing the truth.

And worse yet, Bridget was going to have an even harder time forgetting Chad after that last searing kiss.

Chapter Nine

Miss Gore was not a happy camper. "You should be home."

Chad rolled his eyes as he pressed the speaker button on his cell. "I'm at my brother's house. Isn't family time a good thing?"

There was an audible huff. "Knowing you, there will be alcohol and strippers involved."

Poker and beer—there weren't many things in life better than combining those two. But definitely no naked chicks. Pulling the keys out of the ignition, he considered chucking his phone into the nearby bushes. "We're just playing some poker."

"Just like you were supposed to be going to dinner with your teammate, when in reality you were going out and getting drunk," Miss Gore shot back.

Chad smirked. "Look, if I get drunk and I'm not driving, I'll just crash at my brother Chandler's house. It's no big deal. Chill out."

"I don't like this."

"And I really don't care. Good night, Miss Gore." He cut off her protests by hitting the end button and then turned off his phone.

Damn, if it wasn't for that stipulation in his contract . . .

Shaking his head, he climbed out of his Jeep and headed up the steps. Well-manicured plants and shit lined the sidewalk, which drew a snort from Chad. Chandler, the eldest of the Gamble brood, had the personality of an ox sometimes, but man, his brother had one hell of a green thumb.

Was that a bush of late-blooming roses by the porch? Pansy ass.

An hour later, Chad was kicked back at the card table, watching Chandler deal the cards. Across from Chase, their partner in crime and Maddie's older brother, Mitch, nursed a warm beer.

"Ever since you got married you've started drinking like a grandpa," Chad accused Mitch, scratching at the label on his bottle.

Mitch snorted. "With Lissa's middle-of-the-night cravings, I need to stay sober. I have no idea when she's going to start craving fried chickpeas."

Chad shuddered. "Babies . . ."

Frowning at his cards, Chandler looked up. His longer hair was pulled back in a short ponytail. "Fried chickpeas?"

Mitch nodded. "She dips them in a mixture of ketchup and mustard."

"That's disgusting," Chase murmured, rearranging his cards.

Casting his younger brother a sly look, Chad grinned. "Before you know it, you'll be bouncing little Maddie babies on your knees."

Mitch groaned. "Yeah, can we not talk about that? Seriously?"

"I vote that we don't talk about babies or bouncing them on anyone's knees," Chandler threw in as he tossed some cards out. "It's like playing cards with a bunch of old ladies lately."

Chad snorted as he glanced down at his cards. His hand sucked.

"One of these days, you two will be in the same position as Chase and me." Mitch took a swing of his beer.

"What? Whipped?" Chad asked innocently.

Chandler laughed.

Looking up, Chase's brows rose. "Speaking of whipped . . ."

"You?" Chad offered.

His brother rolled his eyes. "What the hell was going on with you and Bridget today?"

"Bridget?" Mitch frowned. "She works with Maddie, right?"

When Chase nodded and Chad said nothing, Chandler turned to him. "Please tell me you're not screwing Maddie's friend. There has to be at least one woman in the entire city you aren't sleeping with or trying to."

"I haven't slept with her." Not from lack of trying or wanting. "And for the record, there are plenty of women I haven't slept with." Several sets of eyes turned on him in disbelief. Geez. "You know those three women I got pictured with?"

Chandler's brows rose in interest. "Yeah, I think the whole city knows about that."

"I didn't sleep with them, either."

"Whatever," Chase said, tossing a card aside.

Chad laughed. "I'm being serious. Sort of wished I had now, since everyone thinks I did, but shit, I ain't seventeen anymore."

"So what's the deal?" Chase asked, undeterred.

Normally Chad had no problem talking about his extracurricular activities and apparently there were a lot of them, but for some reason, he didn't want to talk about Bridget with his brothers or Mitch, and not because he hadn't had sex with her. He wanted to keep it between the two of them, whatever it was they had between them. She wasn't like the other women—nothing like them. Which was kind of funny considering how he'd met her, but she was different. From what he knew, Bridget wasn't pretentious or hardened and probably didn't give a shit about the fact he played pro ball.

Chad couldn't think of the last time he was with a woman who didn't care about that. Aaand his brothers and Mitch were staring at him.

He slapped his cards down on the table. "Nothing is going on."

"Yeah, I call bull on that shit." Chase eyed him knowingly. "You were getting all kinds of personal with her today."

"When is Chad not up in some woman's personal space?" Mitch asked.

"Ha. Ha."

Chandler smirked.

There were a few grumbled curses as the hand ended and the cards were dealt again. Chase picked right up where he'd left off. "Bridget's a good girl, you know."

He moved his cards around. Full house, baby. "I know."

"Do you? So you know her that well?" Chase countered.

Chad let out a low breath. "I wasn't saying that."

"Uh huh." Chase paused, glancing at Chandler then turning back to him. "Did you sleep with her?"

Lowering his cards, he pinned his younger brother with a look. "Not that it's any of your business, but no, I didn't sleep with her. I already told you that."

"We have a hard—"

"—Time believing me." He cut Chandler off as irritation pricked the back of his neck. "I get it. And seriously, I don't want to talk about Bridget. Move the topic along."

Three sets of curious stares landed on him. It was Chandler who looked the least shocked out of them. He placed two cards down and sat back, smiling to himself. Chad's eyes narrowed.

"Okay." Chase paused for a beat. "But can I give you a word of advice?"

"No."

Chase grinned and went on. "If you make Bridget unhappy, you're gonna make Maddie unhappy. And that's going to make *me* very unhappy."

Chad didn't want to wake up from the dream he was having. Hell no. There was a soft woman underneath him, full of lush curves and hair the color of red wine. She was arching into him, her head thrown back, and he was going so fast and so hard that the bed was slamming into the wall. He never wanted to stop.

The banging got louder until a very loud, very male curse exploded from somewhere upstairs and heavy feet stomped down the stairs, waking him up and ending his amazing dream.

Someone was at his brother's door, and considering the kind of business Chandler ran—a high-profile personal security firm—God only knew who it could be.

All he wanted was to go back to sleep and pick up where he left off. Someone banged on the door again. Chad pried one eye open and grimaced at the bright glare of morning light shining in from the windows behind the couch. Shit. He was blinded and had a hard-on that rivaled marble.

He caught movement out of the corner of one eye and flipped onto his side. Stalking past the couch was Chandler in his boxers and nothing else. "Good morning, sunshine," Chad called out, sitting up.

His brother shot him a nasty look as he went to the front door, wrenching it open so hard, Chad had to wonder how he didn't tear the door right off its hinges.

"Who the fuck are you?" Chandler demanded.

Chad's brows rose as he rubbed his forehead. Man, he hadn't drunk that much last night, but he felt like he'd run his head into a brick wall. Shit. He was getting old.

"I need to see your brother immediately."

An intense throbbing picked up in his left temple and his right eye twitched. Before he could yell not to let her in, Miss Gore brushed past a very pissed off Chandler, stopping only a brief second to give his brother a cursory look before pinning those dark, evil, soulless eyes on him. Chad grabbed the throw off the back of the couch and pulled it over his lap, even though just hearing that woman's voice killed any lingering arousal.

She held a newspaper in her hand. It couldn't be anything about him, since the gossips typically didn't run until Sunday, so he relaxed about a fraction of an inch.

Chandler folded his arms over his chest. "Like I said, who the fuck are you?"

"She's my babysitter I was telling you about," Chad grumbled.

Miss Gore's lips pursed. "I'm his publicist."

"What-the-hell-ever," Chandler said, taking off for the stairs. "I'm going back to bed. It's too early for this shit."

Chad watched his babysitter try and *fail* to not check out his brother. He smirked. Now here he thought Miss Gore was asexual. A door slammed shut a few moments later and Miss Gore got all pissy-faced again.

"To what do I owe this pleasure?" Chad asked, leaning back against the couch.

Without saying a word, she tossed the newspaper at him. It hit his chest. Rolling his eyes, he picked it up and flipped it over. His mouth dropped open. "Oh, shit."

"Those weren't the words I used," she said, standing in front of him. Dressed in a boxy black skirt suit today, she still looked like a damn nun. "You were told to stay away from the women. Can you not make it an entire month?"

Chad could only stare at the headline of the sports section. NATIONALS' PLAYBOY PITCHER MAKES A PLAY ON CONSTITUTION AVE. The picture below was of him and

Bridget under the awning yesterday, kissing. Someone had a good camera because it was a tight shot on their faces.

"The manager of your Club is very disappointed in you *and* in me. That does not make me happy," she said, crossing her arms.

"Does anything make you happy?"

She ignored that. "The fact this is even in the sports section is worse, Chad. I don't think you understand how serious this is."

Chad was too busy staring at the picture to really care. Damn it. He could practically feel Bridget pressed against him right now and that dream he had wasn't helping. He couldn't help but wonder what she would think when she saw the newspaper? Or had she already?

And why did he even care?

"Chad," Miss Gore snapped.

Forgetting the babysitter was still there, he lifted his head and frowned. "What?"

Her frown was so deep he wondered if it would ever fade. "Why did this happen? We've been over this again and again. I cannot repair your image if you keep screwing up."

Why had he done this? "I wanted to kiss her."

Miss Gore blinked and then drew up to her full height, which was a whopping five feet and seven inches. "You wanted to kiss her. So you just normally kiss people when you want to?"

"It's not like she was some random chick on the street."

"Who is this whore, then?"

He was on his feet before he knew it. "You can call me every name you think I deserve, lady, but do not call her that. She is not a whore."

Miss Gore watched him curiously and then smiled tightly. "Interesting."

Throwing the paper onto the couch, he turned and shoved his fingers through his hair. "I haven't slept with her, before you start accusing me of that."

A pause and then, "She doesn't seem like the typical woman you go after."

If he wasn't going to talk to his brothers about Bridget, he sure as hell wasn't going to talk about it with the she-devil. "Look, this isn't a big—"

"It is a big deal." She sat on the other side of the couch, obviously in no mood to leave any time soon. Great. "My wake-up call this morning was not fun. After your manager expressed his vast disappointment, I was given an ultimatum."

Unease soured in his gut. "Are they going to cancel my contract?"

Her expression turned severe. "There was talk of that, yes. There was also talk of firing me."

As much as Chad disliked the woman, a bit of guilt festered within the unease. "I kissed a woman. That's all. They don't even know who she is. What if she was my girlfriend? Would they have a problem with that, too?"

Interest sparked in her dark eyes. "Is she your girlfriend?"

A surprised laugh escaped him. "No. I don't do the dating thing."

"And therein lies the problem. You do the screwing thing. If she were your girlfriend, then they wouldn't have a problem with it. The problem is that in the last six months, you've been pictured with ten or so different women in very compromising positions. And when you're not pictured with a woman, then you're out partying. You're giving the entire Club a bad reputation."

Chad dropped his head into his hands and blew out a deep breath. Rubbing his fingers against his temples, he closed his eyes. "I don't have a drinking problem."

"I don't think you do," she said, surprising him. It seemed like she believed the worst about him when it came to everything else. "But your father did."

His head jerked up, and his eyes narrowed. "Don't even go there."

Miss Gore was unfazed. "All I am saying is that it takes no leap of faith for people to make the jump to a certain conclusion. Your . . . family background plays into this."

Of course it did. Even from the fucking grave his father was screwing things up. Then again, it wasn't really fair to blame everything on dear old Dad. Chad was a grown man and therefore responsible for his own actions. And honestly, he did have his dad to thank for one thing. By watching his father, he learned what not to do with women.

Settle down.

Shit just didn't work out from that point on. And while he didn't have his father's drinking habits, he'd obviously developed his womanizing ones.

"What is the ultimatum?" he asked, so over this conversation.

"I've been given a month to clean you up or your contract is canceled and I'm fired." She paused, brows knitting. "I have never been fired before."

"Shit." He scrubbed his fingers through his hair. "I haven't been with—"

"The newspaper says different, Chad. It's all about perception. And I honestly don't think anything will fix this. The Club has practically given up. They want you, but they don't want your bad press."

He sat back against the cushion and shook his head in disbelief. If he lost his baseball contract, he had no idea what he'd do. He had money to last him a while, but it wouldn't be forever. And he loved the game. Without it, he'd just be going through the motions. And he really didn't want to have to give up his family to go earn a paycheck in New York.

"There is one thing that should work," she said quietly.

Considering he hadn't being doing anything since the babysitter came onboard, or really even before then, he wasn't sure what more he could do other than lock himself up in his house until the start of the season in March. "And what is that?"

"You convince the team and the public that you have a girlfriend." She held up her hand the moment his mouth opened. "The woman you were caught kissing? If we could get her to assume the role of your girlfriend, then I could spin this. The gossips will go crazy thinking you've settled down, but it's the good kind of press. It will show the Club that you've changed your ways and will help repair your public image."

Chad stared at her. "You're joking, right?"

She clasped her hands in her lap. "Does it look like I'm joking? And that's a rhetorical question, so please don't answer. This woman will be the perfect one for it."

Bridget would be perfect for a lot of things. "And why is that?"

"She's not like the women you're normally with. She's average."

His brows slammed down. "She is *not* average." Hell no. She was beyond that. Especially when he thought of her in Leather and Lace, her cheeks flushed prettily and having no idea she was a sheep among wolves.

"In comparison to the women you typically date, she's a lot of things. And most importantly, she's unexpected. She's the kind of woman you settle down with."

And that's exactly why he needed to stay as far away from Bridget as possible.

"No way. I'm not doing this."

"Then you lose your contract," she said simply. "Is that what you want?"

He gritted his teeth. "You know the answer to that."

"Then you shouldn't have a problem with this plan." Miss Gore rose. "I know this is an unconventional plan—"

"Yeah, I'd definitely say it's unconventional. It's also insane. You're asking me and a woman I barely know to pretend to be together?" He shook his head. "This isn't going to work."

"It can."

He snorted. "You'd never get her to agree to it."

Miss Gore's answering smile was that of a player who knew she was about to hit a home run. "I can be rather convincing."

Maybe he was still dreaming, except it had turned into a nightmare. There was no way Bridget would agree to be his girlfriend, and once she turned down Miss Gore's plans, they'd have to move on to something else. What, he didn't know.

"Okay," Chad said. "Have at it."

Chapter Ten

It was the day from hell.

Shell had been blowing up her phone all day. Madison had grilled her like a seasoned homicide detective, repeatedly pointing at the article like it was evidence and, well, it sort of was. And that article?

Under the headline had been a quick write-up about Chad Gamble and a reference to her as the curvaceous—*curvaceous?*—mystery woman locking lips with the "most sought-out bachelor in the major leagues." And then there was the picture that captured the moment with startling detail. Christ, were they using a high-definition camera?

Chad was pressed against Bridget, his hands cupping her face while she grabbed his shirt like she was ready to get it on right then and there.

Oh mercy, there was no way she was living that down.

Everyone had stared at Bridget. Or at least it felt that way. She knew damn well half the floor had seen the article. Poor Robert had looked heartbroken. In the bathroom, Betsy from procurement wanted to give her a high five for crying out loud. To make matters worse, at lunch with Madison, some random blond chick on the street had approached her and felt the need to inform her that Chad was a kiss-and-run kind of guy.

Apparently she was a part of Chad's legion—the bitter side.

Bridget had been mortified as half the patrons waiting outside the taco joint bore witness as Chad's ex-whatever launched into a verbal diatribe about how he was "the best you ever had in bed but the worst out of it" in a high, squeaky voice that had this remarkable ability to carry. Afterward, Bridget wanted to bleach her ears out.

The entire time, Madison looked torn between feeling sorry for her and wanting to laugh. "Sorry," she had said as they headed back to the office. "That's what happens when you date a mini celebrity."

"We're so not dating or doing anything like that," Bridget had said, and then said it again for extra effect.

In the afternoon, someone from the *Washington Post* called to get an interview with her. If being pictured with Chad once led to all of this, she couldn't imagine what dating a man like him would be like. Her entire day had been taken over by this mess, which was just perfect, since he had also consumed her nights.

By the time she got home after work, she was ready to hide under the coffee table with Pepsi or punch someone. After she finished off the carton of leftover Chinese, there was a sturdy knock on her front door. Considering she wasn't late on rent and Shell was out of town on business, she was half afraid to answer the door.

Smoothing her hair back from her face, she went to the door and peered through the peephole. What she saw didn't really relieve her. A very stern face and dark eyes behind glasses stared back, and Bridget had a sudden blast from the past. This lady outside her door reminded her of a teacher who spent more time yelling at her students than teaching them a lick of anything.

Bridget opened the door. "Can I help you?"

The woman before her wore a really boring brown suit skirt set that Bridget wanted to throw neon paint on. The shirt under the suit jacket was white—of course. Color must be a bad, bad thing for this lady. Her gaze traveled down to the sensible pumps and Bridget's internal fashion goddess hung her head in shame. With the mauve shirt she was wearing today and the teal skirt, she must look like a freaking techno rainbow next to this lady.

"Miss Rodgers?" the woman said in a clipped, confident tone.

And she sounded like a teacher. "Yes?"

"My name is Alana Gore." She stepped into Bridget's apartment *without* being invited, holding an oversize bucket purse close to her narrow hips. "I'm Chad Gamble's publicist."

Irritation and about a thousand other emotions raced through Bridget as she closed her door and turned to the lady. Good God, there was no escaping anything Chad-related today. "How did you find out where I live?"

Miss Gore sat down on the edge of the couch, her lips slightly curled as she scanned the bright quilts and pillows on Bridget's couch and chair, and then her gaze landed on the ball of fluff staring out from underneath the coffee table at her. From the look that crossed her face, she was no fan of cats.

Bridget took an immediate dislike to the woman.

"When it comes to finding someone I need to speak with, there are many tools at my fingertips. Take for example, Chad Gamble's brother Chandler; considering what he does for a living, he probably uses the same means as I do." Miss Gore went to place her bag on the floor and then seemed to think twice, as if Bridget's floor was dirty or something, and placed her bag next to her on the couch. "And I really need to speak with you privately."

This was the last thing Bridget wanted or needed at the moment. "This is about the picture in the paper this morning?" When Chad's publicist nodded, Bridget gritted her teeth so hard it was a wonder her molars didn't crack. "Look, that was a one-time-only, freak occurrence—"

"And you're not sleeping with him, and he kissed you just because he wanted to. I know."

"That's what he said?"

Miss Gore frowned. "So you did have sex with him?"

"What? No. I didn't. About the wanting to kiss me—oh, never mind, that part doesn't matter." Bridget shook her head as she sat down in her chair. Pepsi crawled out from under the coffee table, his claws digging into the frayed throw rug. Ears back, he stared up at the stranger. Bridget hoped he didn't pounce on the bag or do something utterly embarrassing, like cough up a mountain-size hairball. "Like I said, it's nothing. So I'm not sure why you're here."

Miss Gore pulled her feet away from Pepsi and folded her ankles. "What kind of relationship do you have with Chad, and please don't say you don't have one, because if so, I'm going to wonder why you allow complete strangers to kiss you."

After the kind of day Bridget had, she wasn't in the mood for this crap. "I really don't see how that is any of your business."

Unfazed, Miss Gore continued. "It is my business as his publicist. Now, he tells me that you two have not had any . . . intimate relationship, but I assume there is more."

"And like I said a few seconds ago, I don't see how what we have or don't is any of your business."

A ghost of a smile appeared. "Are you aware of Chad's reputation?"

Bridget snorted. "Who isn't?"

"I've been brought in by his manager to clean up his image. As you can imagine, that has been a near impossible feat when it comes to his extracurricular activities."

Was that what they were calling being a general man-whore these days?

"I had managed to keep him away from the . . . women for the last month, and then you happened."

The way she said it was like Bridget was a comet that had smacked into Earth. "I'm sorry, but I don't see how his reputation has anything to do with me."

"It does." Miss Gore's perfectly groomed brows knitted as Pepsi came out from under the table. "The only way I can repair his image is if he has a girlfriend."

"O—kay."

"And out of all the women he typically fraternizes with, you don't take your clothes off for a living or make money posing for pictures, and you're not a rich socialite who doesn't know how to use the division table."

Bridget would've laughed at that, because it was true, but a weird feeling was crawling up the back of her neck. "I still have no idea what this has to do with me."

"If Chad were to settle down, even temporarily, with anyone who is *average*, it would do wonders to repair his image. His contract with the Nationals is on the line," Miss Gore explained, and Bridget wasn't sure if she should be insulted by being called average or not. "And that's where I need your help."

Her mouth opened. She hadn't known Chad was close to losing his contract, and she wondered if his brothers knew. Surely Madison would've said something.

"I need you to pretend to be Chad's girlfriend, only for a month." Miss Gore tilted her head to the side. "It would involve a few public appearances with him. Of course, it would not be at your expense at all."

Bridget stared at her. "Are you serious?"

"Yes."

She opened her mouth again, but this time she started to laugh—the deep, belly-shaking kind. "Oh my God . . ."

Miss Gore scowled. "I don't see what's so funny."

"This . . ." Bridget waved her arms. Poor Pepsi's head was swinging back and forth between the two women. "I'm sorry, but this is probably the craziest thing I've ever heard. Pretend to be Chad Gamble's girlfriend? Are you on crack? I don't think anyone in the city would believe that he was capable of being in a relationship with an oven mitt, let alone with a woman."

Miss Gore's lips pursed and then she reached up, took off her glasses, and carefully folded them. "According to my records, you owe around fifty thousand in student loans?"

And that sobered Bridget up real quick. Her laughter died off. "Excuse me?"

"Remember how I said I have many tools at my fingertips?" She held the glasses in her lap. "You went to University of Maryland and graduated with a degree in history; however, without a doctorate in that field, there's not much you can do. You took a job at the Smithsonian, which gets you in the field you love but most definitely doesn't pay the bills. So, as I said, you owe around fifty thousand?"

What in the hell. To know that this uppity woman had obviously been poking around in her personal business and finances, and was a complete stranger, was mortifying. And it all had to do with Chad Gamble, no less. She was pissed as she squirmed in her chair. "That sounds about right."

"What if I could cut you a check for that amount today and all you'd have to do is pretend to be Chad's girlfriend over the next month?"

Bridget leaned forward and then sat back. She snapped her mouth shut. There was no way she could've heard the woman correctly, but she was watching her with a levelheaded stare. "You can't be serious," she finally choked out on a surprised laugh. "There's no way you're being serious."

Miss Gore didn't blink. "I'm being completely serious. You have to understand that my reputation and ability to do my job is on the line. I will do anything to ensure that Chad's image is repaired. *Anything*."

Was she being punked? "You're willing to pay me fifty grand to pretend to be Chad Gamble's girlfriend?"

"That's what I'm saying."

There was a part of Bridget that wanted to jump at the offer. Partly due to the fact she couldn't even comprehend a life where she wasn't sinking under debt. To be out from underneath that mess would be a true blessing. With the extra money from not having to pay those insane loans, she could move into a nicer area and stop the depressing search for a new job. She could sleep a full night without waking up at four a.m., stressing over how she was going to make ends meet. She'd feel like her life was her own again and not owned by debt collectors. And there was also a teeny, tiny part of her that perked up solely based on the fact that she'd be able to see Chad again.

And dear Lord, she didn't even want to look too far into that.

But her pride surfaced. There was no way she could be a part of something like this. Her parents would be rolling over in their graves. It was dirty money. "As helpful as that would be, I'm not a prostitute."

"You wouldn't be required to have sex with him. Frankly, I'd prefer that there was another woman in the city besides me that he hasn't had sex with."

Bridget arched a brow. "You can put this offer in pretty wrappings and tie a bow around it, but I'm accepting money to be someone's girlfriend. No matter which way you look at it, that's a form of prostitution. I'm not that desperate."

"I was afraid you'd say that."

"Then why even approach me with it?"

Miss Gore sighed as she placed her glasses back on, and

her expression hardened. "Well, if you're unwilling to take payment for the service, I have another offer for you."

She started to stand. "I'm not interested. I hope Chad works this out and stays with the Nationals, but this isn't—"

"Please sit," Miss Gore said in such a diplomatic manner Bridget found herself sitting. "You didn't let me finish." She paused and that tight, tense smile appeared. No teeth. "Did you know that upon being hired by the Smithsonian, as with all government-funded jobs, a background and credit check was run? That as a condition of your employment, you must avoid any criminal acts but also keep a clean, healthy credit score?"

A tingle of unease raced down Bridget's spine.

"Defaulting on a student loan can result in termination of your employment even if you've made attempts to make arrears and are currently working with a collection agency." Miss Gore crossed her legs as Pepsi inched closer to her. "Now most employers don't keep up on things like credit checks, but all it would take is one phone call."

Bridget's jaw hit the floor as the unease exploded like a cannon.

"Do you understand, Miss Rodgers?" she asked politely.

"You . . . you wouldn't." Bridget couldn't even believe this woman would do something like that. "That's blackmail."

"Or it's just me doing my civil duty." She shrugged stiffly. "Perhaps you should've accepted the money."

Bridget stared at her a moment and then shot to her feet, sending Pepsi scurrying into the kitchen. "You bitch!"

Miss Gore arched a perfectly groomed eyebrow. "I have

certainly been called worse. This isn't personal. I have a job to do."

"This isn't personal?" Bridget had never hit someone before, but as she curled her hands into fists, she was damn close to doing a meet-and-greet with the woman's face. "You're threatening my job—my livelihood!"

"And Chad's behavior is threatening mine," she replied. "If you want to get angry with anyone . . ." Her gaze dropped to Bridget's hands. "Or hit anyone, take it out on Chad—but not in public, please."

"Get out of my house. Now." Bridget's hands were shaking with the effort to restrain herself.

Instead of standing and leaving like anyone who valued her life would, Miss Gore reached into her bag and pulled out the newspaper. It was open to the gossip section and there it was, the picture of her and Chad on the street, practically eating each other's faces.

Bridget flushed as her lips tingled. Such inappropriate timing.

"You do understand your reputation is also at stake," Miss Gore announced.

Forcing her gaze away from photographic evidence of her attraction to Chad, she took a deep breath. "I don't see how my reputation is affected by this."

Miss Gore picked up the paper and her brows lifted. "Funny thing about photos is how differently they can be perceived from one person to the next, and sometimes all it takes is a different side of the story to be pointed out."

Bridget folded her arms. "What are you getting at?"

She looked up from the paper. "My job as a publicist

requires me to spin things. That's where the whole term *spin doctors* comes from. And I'm really, really good at spinning things. Take this photo, for example. It looks like two people sharing a kiss. Something both of them wanted."

"It was a mistake, but—"

"What it really was doesn't matter. It's all how the public perceives it, and right now they think you're Chad's newest flavor of the week. But what if there was a different side to the story?"

"There isn't a different side to the story. Chad kissed me. I kissed him back." She ran a hand through her hair. "Something I regret for several reasons."

"There's always a different story," Miss Gore said. "Look at this picture—closely. See how you're gripping the front of his shirt, by his shoulders?"

Bridget really didn't want to examine the picture that closely. Bad enough that all she had to do was close her eyes to remember what being kissed by Chad felt like.

"You're also pressed against him," Miss Gore continued. "And a woman of your size has to be fairly strong."

Slowly, Bridget drew in a low, steady breath. Like she was the size of Jabba the Hut or something.

"To me, it looks like you're grabbing Chad and forcing him to kiss you."

"What?" she shrieked. "That's—"

"Celebrities like Chad do have many women—sad, lonely, and slightly overweight women—who do approach him quite often. It's no stretch of the imagination to assume that he has a stalker or two." Miss Gore glanced at the photo. "To me it looks like you accosted him on the street and forced yourself on him."

Red-hot fury slammed into Bridget. "I would never do something like that! How dare you insinuate—"

"I don't dare, Bridget. I will do it. You'll give me no other choice. It's the only way I can cover up his latest mess-up, which is *you*. Perhaps you should've avoided his advances." Miss Gore smoothed her hands over her skirt. "It's unsavory and quite a bitch move. I agree. But that doesn't change the fact that I will release a public statement accusing you of stalking Chad Gamble and forcing yourself on him."

"I'm going to hit you—put all of my *considerable* weight behind it," Bridget said, eyeing the heavy lamp beside the couch. How much prison time would she get if she whacked it over the bitch's head?

Miss Gore didn't look too concerned. "All you have to do is pretend to be dating Chad. That's all. You'll keep your job and your reputation. And let's be honest here, dating Chad is surely going to increase *your* dating potential later on. Every man in the city is going to want to know what you have that hooked a playboy like Chad."

If she wasn't so pissed off, she'd be offended by those statements. What she wanted to do was kick her foot so far up this lady's rear that she'd need a doctor to remove it.

Bridget turned away and stalked behind the chair she'd been sitting in, taking several deep breaths. Her apartment was shoebox sized, but now she really felt it—the walls closing in. She was trapped. There was no doubt in her mind that Miss Gore would do exactly what she threatened. Bridget would lose her job and end up looking like a psycho in the process. And just like her pride had refused to let her accept money for being Chad's pretend girlfriend, pride refused to allow her to be labeled as some kind of fatal attraction wannabe with a weight problem. She could see the gossips now. The things they'd say about her . . .

She swallowed hard, but the sudden lump of messy, ugly emotions didn't budge. Damn Chad for dragging her into this mess.

Facing Miss Gore, Bridget sent her a death glare. "I think this is disgusting, and I'm sure there's a special place in hell for you, Miss Gore, but you've left me no other choice."

A look of remorse flickered across Miss Gore's otherwise impassive expression, but it was so quick that Bridget soon doubted she even saw it. Miss Gore placed a card on the coffee table as she stood. "I expect you to be at the address provided tomorrow evening at seven to go over the ground rules with Chad. Wear something . . . nice." That tight, fake smile again. "You will have a late dinner with Chad at Jaws."

Jaws was an upscale seafood joint that Bridget couldn't even afford to walk past. Letting out a shaky breath, she watched the publicist/dictator stroll toward the front door.

Miss Gore stopped and looked over her shoulder. The woman's spine was straight as a nail under the suit. "Don't be late, Bridget."

Bridget did the only thing she could do in this situation that wouldn't end with her doing a life stint in prison. She flipped the woman off.

With both hands.

Chapter Eleven

Chad had been stunned into silence when Miss Gore called and informed him Bridget had agreed to pretend to be his girlfriend. He'd been positive she would've laughed his publicist right out of town, and they'd be scrambling for another way to repair an image he'd been partly responsible for. Maybe he'd been right about Bridget all along, and she was no different than the other women who wanted to be with him for the attention.

That was a damn shame.

"You're pacing." Miss Gore's voice grated on his every last damn nerve.

Chad stopped and stared out the window overlooking a manicured park that split the teeming avenue.

From the sectional couch, Miss Gore sighed. "You should be thrilled by this development."

The only thing that thrilled him was the fact he'd get to see Bridget again without having to seek her out. How fucked up was that?

"I must say your place is by far nicer than Bridget's. She has a thing for . . . color. Her walls are blue, red, and yellow. The pillows on her couch have every color of the rainbow in them. It was like being in an episode of *Sesame Street*."

A slow smile pulled at his lips as he leaned against the windowpane and folded his arms.

"And she has a cat." Miss Gore shuddered. "A cat the size of a small dog."

Chad wasn't big on cats, being more of a dog person himself, but apparently he found them more tolerable than Miss Gore. There was a knock on the door, soft and almost hesitant. He turned from the window and thrust his fingers through his hair. The clock on the wall said it was a minute till seven.

"You going to get that?" Miss Gore asked.

He shot the woman a look. "You invited her. This was your idea."

"And that kind of attitude isn't going to work. Get the door."

Chad balked at her demanding tone and had half a mind to toss her out into the hallway. The only thing stopping him was that his *life* was on the line. Crossing the living room, he passed the kitchen and went into the foyer. He took a deep breath and opened the door.

Bridget.

Her hair was down, like it had been the night in the club, falling in waves around her face. A faint pink blush stained her cheeks, causing tiny freckles he hadn't noticed before to stand out over her cheeks and the bridge of her nose. Since they were supposed to go out later or some shit like that, she was wearing another demure sweater dress in deep green. The black knee boots with their pointy toes seemed toned down for her, but she looked good.

She looked really good.

Bridget's bottle-green eyes were focused straight ahead, but she wasn't seeing him. "Sorry if I'm late," she said.

"You're not." He stepped aside, and for the first time in a long, long freaking time, he felt nervous. "Would you like something to drink?"

"The strongest liquor you have," she said, placing her clutch on the kitchen counter as she brushed past him. He inhaled deeply, lust stirring at the smell of jasmine. There was the color, he realized as his gaze fell to the clutch. The thing was blue, red, purple, and green.

Chad turned to the cabinet, but Miss Gore appeared out of nowhere. "I do not think alcohol is a good idea right now."

Bridget's spine stiffened as she turned to the woman. "If you expect me to go through with this, I need a drink. A really hard drink."

Wondering if he should feel insulted or not, he grabbed a glass and a bottle of Grey Goose from the cabinet. "Tonight sounds like it's going to be fun." He poured Bridget a glass and handed it to her. "Can't wait to get started."

Bridget's eyes narrowed on him as her fingers brushed his. She jerked back, and clear liquor sloshed over the rim, running down her fingers. Man, he wanted to lick that right off.

He doubted Miss Prissy would approve.

And, by the way Bridget was not looking at him, she wouldn't, either.

Putting the vodka back, he closed the cabinet door. "So we're doing dinner?" he asked, wanting to get this show on the road.

"We need to cover some ground rules first," Miss Gore said, gesturing back to the living room like she owned the damn apartment. "Follow me?"

Bridget moved past Miss Gore, and he'd swear the temperature in the room dropped by the look she'd given the woman. At least they could bond over their mutual dislike of his publicist.

He watched Bridget sit on the edge of the couch, his gaze glued to that lovely ass of hers. He chose to stand back at the window, but this time the scenery was a lot more interesting inside his place.

"Before you say a word," Bridget said, holding up a hand as she twisted toward Miss Gore, "I want your promise that this will only be a month."

Chad's brows shot up.

Jumping in before Chad could open his mouth, his publicist nodded. "It would be a little over a month—a few days. Basically until New Year's Day."

Bridget lowered her hand and took a nice, long, and healthy gulp of vodka. Now his eyes narrowed on her. "Do you think you can make it that long?" he asked sardonically.

"I think I'll need to develop a drug habit to get through this," she said, smiling sweetly.

Miss Gore stepped forward. "Actually, I would advise against that."

Bridget's brows rose as she took another drink of the vodka. "Sorry, but this is all new to me."

"Well, I've never had anyone pretend to be my girlfriend, so I'm in the same boat as you."

She glanced at him but quickly looked away. "What are the ground rules?"

Miss Gore's gaze traveled between the two, her eyes sharp. "No public intoxication or drug use."

Chad folded his arms, exasperated. "I don't do drugs."

"That last part was meant for her."

Now it was Bridget's turn to look riled. "I'll try to refrain from doing my daily hit of crack."

Chad barked out a short laugh, but Miss Gore was not amused. "You two will need to be believable. I suggest that you do not tell any of your friends or family about this arrangement. If this were to get out to the press, we'd all look like fools."

"Then maybe we should find another way," Chad suggested.

Bridget's gaze dropped to her half-full glass. "I agree."

"There is no other way. You've made your bed with Bridget and now you get to roll around and lie in it. Moving on." Miss Gore straightened her glasses. "You must be convincing to the public. No arguing. You have to act like you like each other, and given the fact that you two shared a very public kiss, that shouldn't be too hard."

A pretty flush crawled over Bridget's cheeks. "Can we not talk about that?"

Chad had been entertaining a quick fantasy of tracing the rush of blood with his fingers, mouth, and tongue. "Oh, you're going to start the whole 'I'm not attracted to you' thing again?"

"Just because *you* kissed me doesn't mean I'm attracted to you," she shot back.

Oh, here the fuck we go again. "*You* kissed me back."

"I didn't have much of a choice." Her hand had tightened around the glass. "Just like I don't have much of a choice right this second."

The way Bridget said that made it sound like she was about to take a job shoveling pig shit. "It could be worse. I hear I'm a pretty good catch."

"Yeah, when you were named Sexiest whatever alive *last year*, when you were still relevant."

"Ouch." Chad's brows shot up, and he laughed, genuinely amused. "I'll be expecting a written apology when I'm named again this year."

Bridget eyed him over the rim of her glass. "If that happens, then I seriously question the taste of American women."

He remembered easily how great *she* had tasted. "If I recall correctly, you've—"

"Children," snapped Miss Gore. "You two kissed. We've established that. All right? Obviously there is some sort of attraction between you, but I cannot have you two behaving like bickering children in public."

Bridget glanced down at her glass. "I need more vodka."

"Aw, come on," Chad drawled.

Miss Gore's sigh was a work of art and managed to silence both of them. "How did you two meet?"

Since Bridget said nothing, he decided it was up to him to come out with the truth. "We met at a bar about a month ago. She obviously knew who I was and my family, since she works with my brother's girlfriend. I didn't know this." And truth be told, he wasn't sure whether, if he had known, it would've changed anything that night. "Anyway, we spent a few hours together."

Bridget had gone very quiet during this and seemed relieved when he hadn't elaborated any further, and he wasn't going to, no matter how many questions Miss Gore asked. Luckily, she nodded and moved on.

"You two will need to act as if you're in love." Miss Gore rocked back on her heels. "You should definitely hold her hand while you're out. And— What?" She frowned at his raised eyebrows. "You know, place your hand in hers."

"I know how to hold hands," Chad growled, and Bridget snickered. He sent her a look, and her eyes rolled. "And contrary to popular belief, I know how to date someone."

"Now that *is* shocking." Bridget took another drink. "I thought you only knew how— Hey!"

Chad shot forward, moving so fast that he knew he'd startled her. Very carefully, he took the glass from her. "I think you've had enough."

She gave him a dirty look. "Not nearly enough."

While he thought her feisty responses were rather cute—and he wasn't sure when *cute* became a part of his vocab—his ego was starting to get a little bruised.

Miss Gore smoothed a hand over her tightly pulled back hair. "I think we could do about three public appearances during the week, plus a night out on Saturday. If the press catches on, you may be required to spend the night here, Bridget, to make it believable."

"What?" Her eyes had gone wide. "I didn't agree to that."

His publicist's lips thinned. "There are guest rooms here, and you're both adults. Start acting like it."

Bridget's cheeks flushed. "I really don't like you."

Chad bit back a smile.

"You don't have to like me," Miss Gore responded coolly. "There is also a Christmas event hosted by the Nationals you'll be expected to attend together. With the very public dates and that event, it should calm down the press or at least switch to more appropriate write-ups on your personal life, Chad."

"What about after the New Year?" Bridget asked. "If we 'break up' afterward, wouldn't that be bad press for him?"

He was kind of surprised that Bridget even cared if it was, but then again, he didn't really know why she agreed to do this in the first place. He'd thought for sure she'd have told Miss Gore to take a flying fuck and slammed the door in her face. Only a true wacko who craved attention would want to join this three-ring circus. Chad frowned.

"There will be no public statement, but eventually the press will catch on to you two not being seen together. At that point, I will release a statement that you two remain good friends." Her dark gaze landed on him. "After this month is over, it doesn't mean you go back to your old ways."

"I figured as much," he said dryly, wondering if the woman thought he was an oversexed idiot.

"If by the end of the year, the Club is happy with the changes in your behavior, your contract won't be canceled." She paused, and he knew she was thinking about her own reputation, not that he could blame her. "And hopefully you will take this as a learning experience."

What he'd learned so far was that the press greatly over-exaggerated the truth and generally sucked ass.

Miss Gore went over a couple more ground rules, all really just common sense, and a general breakdown on what you do when you like someone. If it hadn't been for the fact that Miss Gore must've believed he was an imbecile when it came to women, he would've laughed.

When it seemed like his publicist had run out of things to say, he wanted to ram his head into the wall. "So are we ready to do this?"

Miss Gore nodded, but he didn't really care what she thought. The other woman was sitting on the couch, pale and stiff, her fingers clenched in her lap. As he stared at her, he felt a pang of regret. He had no idea why she was doing this, but it was clear she really didn't want to. It was fucked up, but the more upset she appeared the happier it made him. He hadn't liked the idea of Bridget as attention seeking. Now he wanted to call this whole thing off. It wasn't right. His career shouldn't be more important than her comfort.

But then Bridget stood and looked at him, and he was immediately drawn into those green, green eyes. Everything he was thinking was thrown out the damn window, replaced by the need to see those eyes heated until they looked like shining emeralds.

"You ready?" she said, her voice surprisingly steady.

Damn, he was ready, in more ways than one, but he also wanted to run. And Chad had never wanted to run before.

Chapter Twelve

Bridget half expected Miss Gore to play chaperone on their first "date," so when it appeared they were doing this all on their own she was caught between being relieved and nervous. She hated how bitchy she had been toward Chad, really embarrassed by it, but this was *his* fault.

The ride to the upscale restaurant had been quiet. Not so much awkward as it was tense. Neither of them knew what to say. What kind of icebreaker did you use when you were pretending to date each other?

Bridget was never good at pretending anything. Once in high school, she had tried out for the annual play and was so bad during the auditions, she had run off the stage. There had to have been another woman in the long list of the ones he'd been seen with recently who would've been a better choice for this part.

As they pulled up to valet and her door was opened, she couldn't help but notice how different they were. First, she wouldn't even attempt to have her busted-ass Camry parked by valet. Secondly, she didn't eat at places like this. If she had to know what the correct fork was to use for her salad or spoon for her soup, she was so screwed.

Chad appeared in front of her, offering his hand like the dutiful boyfriend. There was a half smile on his face, part teasing and part smug. She stared at him and the third reason why she shouldn't have been on the list was so glaringly obvious.

Dressed in dark jeans and a V-neck sweater that clung to his trim sides and hard stomach, he looked like he'd stepped right off the pages of a *GQ* magazine. Even his hair, artfully messy, looked like it had been professionally styled for this event.

Bridget tilted her head back and met those incredibly blue eyes. She felt like a troll standing next to him. Not because she thought of herself as that ugly or that fat. Her self-esteem wasn't completely in the shitter, but she was realistic. Guys like him didn't date girls like her.

This whole thing was just going to end in humiliation for her.

Chad took the initiative and threaded his fingers through hers. "While I like that you're just standing there and staring at me, we should go in. You're not wearing a coat."

Bridget flushed and started to pull her hand free, but he held on.

"Nuh-uh," he murmured, voice light and playful. "Miss Gore said we must hold hands, and I'm following the rules."

Her eyes narrowed. "Now you're going to listen to her?"

A look of pure innocence crossed his face. "I'm going to be a good boy . . . right now."

The heat that intensified had nothing to do with the fact she'd been caught staring at him. What she'd seen so far of "naughty Chad" was probably nothing to what he was actually capable of.

Nothing out of the ordinary happened on the way into Jaws, but Bridget was surprised by the fact the place didn't smell of seafood. They were seated immediately in the back, at a table lit by a single candle.

Heads turned like they did in the movies as he pulled out the chair for her and she sat. Being wholly conscious of her surroundings, she told herself not to look, to act as if this were totally normal, but she quickly scanned the restaurant and found that half of the tables were staring at them. Some of the expressions were just curious. Others were staring at him in open wonder and awe. Then, among them, were looks of confusion as their gazes bounced back and forth between the two of them, as if they couldn't figure out how they were having dinner together.

She took a deep breath. "Everyone is staring."

"You'll get used to it." He took the seat across from her and gave her a little smile, a tight one that showed no teeth and didn't reveal those dimples of his. "Or they'll find something else to stare at."

She hoped they found something soon, since her face was flaming a thousand shades of red. "Did you call ahead?"

Chad unfolded his napkin. "No. But they make sure I always get a good seat."

Her brows rose. The restaurant was pretty packed, so they had to have kept certain seats open for "special" clients. She couldn't remember the last time she was seated immediately at a nice restaurant.

A waiter appeared at their table, dressed in a white shirt and black pants. "Chardonnay okay?" Chad asked.

Bridget nodded, almost wishing for something harder.

As the waiter bowed and rushed off to fulfill the order, she searched desperately for something to say, anything, but her mind emptied. She stared at the white votive candle hopelessly, until her eyes must've crossed because Chad chuckled deeply.

She forced her gaze up. "What?"

"Nothing," he replied, smiling slightly. "It's just that before this, we talked for three hours straight without a moment of awkwardness."

Bridget bit down on her lower lip. "We did."

"So what's changed?" He leaned back and the sweater stretched over his broad shoulders.

"Well, the fact that both of us are pretending to be dating is different." Bridget glanced over and saw someone at a few round tables over holding a cell phone up. "And I think someone is taking our picture."

Chad smirked. "It'll be on Facebook within seconds."

"Really?"

He nodded.

"Does this happen all the time?"

"Yep."

God, she couldn't imagine living like that. Then again, she was living like that now, and she really hoped her hair looked great and she didn't end up with a double chin from holding her head down. The waiter appeared, and she quickly scanned the menu while Chad ordered some kind of surf and turf.

"I'll have the scallops," she said, folding the menu and handing it back.

The waiter bowed once more and then dashed off again.

Bridget watched him, wondering if he always moved that fast.

"Is that all you're going to eat?" Chad asked.

She faced him and wished he weren't so damn good-looking. Couldn't he at least have a snaggletooth? Was that really too much to ask for? "That's enough."

Chad looked doubtful but wisely didn't pursue that particular road to hell. "So, I'm dying to know something."

"I'm afraid to ask." She picked up her glass and took a sip of wine.

"When we met at the club, why didn't you tell me you knew Maddie and Chase?"

She cringed inwardly at that question. "I . . . I didn't think it was a big deal at the time."

"I'd think that's one of the first things people would say." As he spoke, he ran a fingertip along the rim of his wine-glass in a slow, idle circle that drew her attention. "Especially since there is no way that Maddie hadn't spoken about me."

"Maybe she didn't talk about you." Bridget forced her gaze away from his fingers. "Did you ever think about that?"

His laugh was low and sent a shiver down her arms. "Oh, I know Maddie would've talked about me."

"Your ego never ceases to amaze me."

Chad smiled, and it appeared he was about to follow that up with a real winner of a response that would've reluctantly amused Bridget, but the waiter arrived and steaming plates were placed on their tables. The moment the waiter backed away, Chad was right back on track.

"So, why didn't you say anything?"

Bridget dropped the napkin in her lap and tugged it into

place with quick movements. No way was she going to admit to the real reason. "I didn't think it mattered."

"Just like you're not attracted to me?"

She sighed. "Back to that again?"

"No." He smiled and—her little heart jumped—there were the dimples. "You're just a terrible liar. "

Truthfully, she was.

Chad cut his medium-rare steak as she chased a buttery scallop across her plate. "The answer is yes," he said.

Her fork froze. "To what?"

He peered up through thick lashes. "Even if I knew you worked with Maddie and you knew my brother, I still would've taken you home."

Bridget's heart did another cartwheel as she stared at him. How had he known the truth? She didn't want to look too closely into that. Silence fell between them and as they ate, she noticed he barely drank any of the wine and stuck to the water while he ate with a zest she envied.

She looked up when someone approached the table. It was a cute brunette, barely into her twenties, who wore the cutest red dress with cap sleeves. Her cheeks were flushed as Chad put down his silverware.

"I don't mean to interrupt you and your friend," the girl said. "But I'm here with my girlfriend." She nodded over to a table where a blond-haired girl beamed. "And I just had to tell you that you're the main reason why I watch baseball."

Bridget's lips pursed. Was there any wonder Chad had a gigantic ego?

"Thank you," he said, smiling. "Good to know I'm doing my part in spreading the love of the game."

Oh. Eye. Roll.

The girl bit down on a glossy lower lip and placed her hand on the table beside Chad. It was then when Bridget realized she had a piece of paper in her hand. "Call me, okay? Anytime."

Bridget wondered if she was visible, and she also wanted to dash under the linen-covered table or recreate a jungle scene and take the chick out, which made no sense.

Chad's smile didn't fade. "That's really kind of you, but I'm not available."

Eyes widening to epic proportions, Bridget went very still as the brunette glanced from Chad to her.

"This is Bridget," Chad continued. "My girlfriend."

A dumbfounded look crossed the girl's face and her mouth opened, but she closed it. Murmuring an apology, she went back to her table, where she immediately started whispering to her friend.

Bridget squeezed her eyes shut.

"Well, that will probably also go out on Twitter," he said, and she opened her eyes. "What?" he teased. "My relationship status is apparently big news."

Taking a drink of the wine, she told herself to just keep her mouth shut. Her mouth didn't listen. "When the picture of us hit the newspaper—"

"A good day for you, I'm sure."

She took a deep breath. "Some lady approached me on the street as I tried to go to lunch and told me you were good in bed but not out of it."

"Oh." He arched a brow. "Well, the 'in bed' part is true and it's been—"

"This isn't funny."

"Whoa—why the attitude toward me?"

Was he for real? There was a whole buttload of reasons. Leaning forward, she kept her voice down. "You've successfully hijacked my life in a matter of hours."

Chad frowned. "I haven't done anything."

"Really?" she hissed. "Did you slip and fall into bed with three girls and there just happened to be someone there to take a picture?"

His eyes flashed a deep denim blue. "That damn photo. I didn't sleep with them."

Bridget didn't know if she should laugh or throw her wine in his face. "Yeah, said no man ever."

His eyes rolled. "Why doesn't anyone believe me? I don't get it."

Did he really think she was that dumb? "All of this because you kissed me—"

"And you enjoyed it."

"That's not the point, you jerk." Bridget glanced around. Surprisingly, no one was paying attention to them at the moment. "I have no control over my life now because of you."

Chad inched forward, too, until only the flickering candle separated their mouths. "And I'll say it again—how is this my fault?"

"Is anything you do your fault?" she demanded.

"Whatever. You didn't have to agree to do this."

"I had no choice. Your publicist from hell blackmailed me." Surprise flickered over Chad's face, and Bridget nearly fell out of her chair. "What? Did you think I'd just agree to this?"

"Well, I mean, come on, I *am* Chad Gamble." Then he smirked.

She was seconds away from throwing her plate of scallops in his face. "God, there are no words sometimes. I know I'm not like the women you normally go out with, but I'm not desperate enough to have to pretend I have a boyfriend."

A strange look replaced the surprise and he leaned back, folding muscular—she was so not looking at them—arms across his chest. "Yeah, you're not like them."

Out of nowhere, a sharp pain sliced across her chest. She jerked back and tried to swallow the sudden lump in her throat. "Can we call it a night now? I'm sure your adoring public has had their fill."

The expected cocky response was absent as he signaled the waiter and picked up the check. He did the boyfriend thing. Stood and took her hand in his warm one, and that damn lump ended up between her breasts now.

Outside, she could see people waiting. Someone must've updated some social site or made a phone call. Chad went into full acting mode the moment they stepped into the late November air. A camera lightbulb flashed, and he dropped her hand, slipping an arm over her shoulders.

He bent his head, grazing her cheek with his jaw. A fine shiver danced across her shoulders, and she hated how her body wanted to lean into his, just as everyone expected that she would.

His chin continued to her temple, and she sucked in a sharp breath. "You could try to relax," he murmured. "Because right now, you look like you want to run."

"That's because I want to run." But she forced a smile.

Another bulb flashed, and Chad pressed a kiss to her cheek. Someone had better give that boy an Oscar. "That's kind of mean."

As they waited for the valet to bring his car around, several more flashes blinded Bridget. "It's the truth."

"Uh huh," he murmured as he slid his hand off her shoulder and down to the small of her back, causing her to jerk. "What is Miss Gore blackmailing you with?"

The truth formed on the tip of her tongue, but she closed her mouth. The last thing she wanted to share with Chad was how pitifully broke she was, that she could lose her job because of it. "It's none of your business."

"Hmm, must be juicy if you don't want to share." He stepped in closer and placed his other hand on her hip.

Bridget stiffened. "What are you doing?"

"Giving them something to put in the newspaper."

"You don't—"

Chad kissed her again.

It was nothing like the one on the side of the street or those in his bedroom. This one started off as a slow, tantalizing sweep of his lips. She forced her lips closed and to remain still in his arms. They could pretend to be dating, but this—the kissing—was so not a part of the plan.

In the wave of flashing lights, Chad growled low in his throat, and Bridget shuddered. "Don't fight what you know you want," he said in a low, seductive tone.

"You have no idea what I want," she replied, but damn it, what she wanted was him between her thighs. But not like this—not when they were *pretending*.

His lips made another sweep, but this time he caught her lower lip with his teeth, and she gasped. Heat exploded through her every last nerve ending and like before, her body won out over her head. He took full advantage, slipping his tongue in, taking complete control within seconds. His hand traveled up to the nape of her neck and held her there as his mouth was hot and demanding, slanted across her lips. At that moment, she wasn't going anywhere anytime soon. Oh Lordie Lord no. Her knees were weak and the muscles in her belly did tight, funny things.

The kiss went on, and it was how it should be. Not rushed in the heat of the moment. Not an act to prove that there was attraction. It was an unhurried, playful, and measured seductive assault that left her senses reeling.

Chad lifted his mouth a hairsbreadth from hers. "Tell me how Miss Gore got you to do this."

"It wasn't blackmail," she said, toying with her bracelet. Then she remembered what Miss Gore had said to her and wasn't sure what provoked her to say what she did next. Maybe it was how he said she wasn't like the girls he normally went for. Or maybe it was how breathless and dazed the kiss had left her and how she knew that kind of response was going to get her into nothing but trouble. "Going out with you is really going to increase the dating pool for me in the future, right? Guys are going to want to know what I have that caught your interest."

Chad stared at her a long moment and then said, "Right."

The valet appeared with Chad's keys in his hand before she could take the words back. God, that came out sounding as horrible as it had when Miss Gore had said it.

She was barely aware of the cameras going off when the passenger door was held open for her and she slid into the front seat. In a daze, she placed her fingers to her lips as Chad loped around the front of the car and climbed in.

The playfulness was gone from his movements when he got into the Jeep. His jaw was set in a hard, firm line. He didn't look at her. He didn't say anything, in fact, as he shifted the gears into drive.

Bridget turned away from him, having no idea what to say. She wanted to apologize but wasn't sure there really was a point. And besides, for a moment, a blind, stupid moment when his mouth had been against hers, she had forgotten what was really going on. That she wasn't the kind of woman Chad preferred and that he, like her, had no choice in this.

This was so wrong, and she really had no idea how they could do this without tearing each other's heads off. Or how long she could last knowing every hand held, every kiss for the cameras, was faked.

Chapter Thirteen

"You're dating Chad?" shrieked Madison.

Bridget hated lying to her, but she knew if she told the truth, Madison would tell Chase. "Yeah, something like that."

Buzzing back and forth between their two desks, Madison was like a cracked-out hummingbird. "I can't believe it."

"Neither can I," Bridget muttered dryly. After their first dinner last night, she'd gone home in a mood worse than when she'd left. And she'd still been starving.

"I mean, not that I can't picture you with Chad. I can. But I just can't picture him settling down." She paused halfway between the desks and frowned.

"Then again, I couldn't picture Chase settling down, either, but he did."

"This is nothing like you and Chase." Bridget started color-coding her Highlighters. "Anyway, did we get final numbers on the catering yet?"

Madison was not derailed by the more important conversation. They'd been working on the Gala since *last* February. The damn thing had consumed both their lives and now

Chad was consuming hers. "What do you mean, it's not like Chase and me?"

Moving the pink Highlighters next to the green ones, she sighed. "It's just not serious. Not like you guys."

Madison stopped in front of Bridget's desk and propped her hands on her hips. "Okay, when's the last time you had a boyfriend or was dating someone?"

"Uh . . ."

"Exactly," Madison said and then resumed her pacing. "You dating Chad *is* serious. It can't be anything less than serious. Did you see the *Washington Post* online this morning? There were pictures of you two kissing." She picked a pen up off her desk and threw it at Bridget. "Kissing! I'm pretty sure it's on CeleBuzz, too. I can't believe you didn't tell me!"

Bridget picked up the pen and cringed. "I just didn't think anything was going to come out of it."

Madison stared at her, nose wrinkled in concentration. "God, are you ready for all of this, Bridget? It's going to be insane. People are going to start following you around. Oh! I can pretend to be your assistant!"

Bridget rolled her eyes.

"And we can double date."

Oh, dear . . .

"And Chad always comes to the Daniels Family Christmas Dinner Extravaganza, which you never come to even though I've invited you every year, you hooch." Madison clamped her hands together. "Now you can't get out of it."

She so wasn't a fan of the holidays, and honestly, it hurt

to see Madison making happy plans. She was going to be so disappointed when, at the beginning of the year, Chad and Bridget went their separate ways.

Madison finally settled down, and Bridget opted to eat in for lunch. She was half afraid to visit any of the local joints. Just before three in the afternoon, their office door opened and a delivery guy stood there, awkwardly carrying four dozen red roses.

Four dozen roses.

Wow. Last night must've been amazing for Chase to send Madison an arrangement like that.

Bridget went back to staring at her computer screen. She needed to e-mail the catering company if they hadn't gotten a definite amount back for the—

"Is there a Bridget Rodgers here?"

Lifting her chin, her gaze landed on the flower guy. Confused, she glanced over at a grinning Madison. "Um, that's me."

The man smiled as he moved toward her desk. She hastily cleared off a little section on the corner. "Someone must really love you," the man said, placing the vase down. "Have a nice day."

Bridget stared at the delivery guy as he strode out of her office, and then her gaze fell back to the roses. Holy crap . . .

Miss Gore must've ordered them or made Chad do it. That could be the only reason why they were for her, but they . . . they were beautiful.

"Is there a card?"

She looked up, barely able to see Madison from behind the forest of stems. There was a card, tucked neatly between a dewy green stem and baby's breath. Very carefully, she pulled the card out and slid open the little envelope.

Written in pretty calligraphy was a short message that might not have told why the flowers were sent but definitely who had sent them.

I'm still very relevant.

Chad.

As she stared at the little card, there was no fighting the slow smile that crept over her face. Yeah. He was still relevant.

After getting an earful from Chase about "dating" his woman's good friend and then putting up with Chandler's snide-ass comments about going the way of every guy around them and settling down, Chad was ready to bang his head through the wall when his cell went off.

Expecting the hourly check-in from Miss Gore, because who knew what kind of trouble he could get into in his own apartment, he swiped the cell off his kitchen counter. The text wasn't from his babysitter. Oh, no, it was Bridget. His publicist all but forced them to exchange numbers before they went out to dinner.

Thank you for the roses. They're beautiful.

About two seconds later another text came through. *Still not relevant, though.*

A smile hit his lips, and it was a good thing his brothers had left by then because he was sure he looked like a dumbass. He liked her response—a lot—and he also liked that she didn't text like a sixteen-year-old girl.

Like most of the women he hung out with.

Chad put the phone back on the counter and went to the fridge, grabbing the chicken he'd marinated earlier. Dumping it on the Foreman grill, he poked the breasts around with a fork until they were placed perfectly in the middle.

He closed the lid. Juices sizzled.

And then he glanced over the counter at his phone.

He turned back to the counter and tossed the fork onto the countertop. Rocking back on his heels, he stared at the grill. That lasted about thirty seconds.

"Hell," he muttered, spinning toward his phone.

Picking it up, he tapped the screen and stared at the message. There were no plans tonight, but tomorrow was supposed to be a movie. He hadn't gone to a theatre since he was in high school. Movie premieres not included.

Technically, he had no reason to be in contact with Bridget, since this was kind of like a day off. And he really hadn't had a reason for sending her flowers other than . . . he'd wanted to.

Okay, there was more to it.

Turning around, he leaned against the counter and stretched out the kink in his neck.

It wasn't because of the kiss they'd shared. Although just thinking about that kiss got him hard as a rock, but it was what she'd said. That she'd agreed to pretend to be his girlfriend because it would help out her dating after him.

What. The. Fuck.

First off, he doubted she needed the help. Secondly, he wasn't too keen on being a stepping-stone. So he sent her roses. Strange response to something like that, sure, but he doubted she was thinking about her future boyfriends now.

He sent her a text back. *Glad you liked the flowers.*

Before he could put the phone back down, his fingers just kept on typing. *And glad you liked the kiss.*

He dropped the cell and checked his chicken. About a minute later, his phone went off and he piddled around the kitchen for another three minutes before he went to check it.

I never said I liked the kiss.

A grin pulled at his lips as he sent a message back. *You didn't have to. I know.*

The response was immediate. *Do I need to remind you that YOU kissed ME both times?*

Chad tipped his head back and laughed, but he checked his chicken before responding. Otherwise it looked like he was just standing in the kitchen, holding his phone, which he was.

After slopping the grilled bird on a plate and cutting it up into tiny pieces like he was preparing it for a child, he sent another text. *Do I need to remind you that YOU enjoyed it both times?*

The response was pretty quick. *Le sigh.*

Chuckling to himself, he carried his food to the couch and ate his dinner while watching the evening news. Exciting stuff there. He let his food settle before he hit the treadmill in his library for the obligatory evening run. Afterward, he stripped off his sweat-soaked shirt and unbelievably did a load of laundry.

Each time he passed his phone, he looked at it. Each time it rang, there was a stupid feeling in his stomach. By the time he got done cleaning the guest bathroom down-stairs and taking a shower, he found himself holding his cell. It was past ten, probably too late to call, not that he was planning to call Bridget. Miss Gore had already set plans for the movie date. He was to pick her up at her place and blah blah.

Once in bed, his fingers got the best of him. He texted: *Good night, Bridget.*

Two minutes later he got the same kind of response, and then he put the phone on the farthest corner of the bedside table. Having an early morning with his off-season trainer, he needed to sleep.

An hour later, he was still staring at the ceiling, tired, but his mind started messing with him, bringing forth images of Bridget against that very wall of his bedroom, her head thrown back, breasts jutted out as he watched her from his knees. He breathed in deeply and swore he could still taste her sharp arousal.

He threw the sheet off and moved his hand down his stomach. Palming his heavy erection, his back bowed clear off the mattress. Jesus. He hadn't been strung this tight since college.

His hand stroked down his throbbing shaft and his eyes fell shut. Immediately, the image of Bridget formed in his mind, except he was standing against the wall and she was on her knees. Her mouth replaced his hand and yep, that was all it took. His release pounded down his spine and his hips punched up at his own hand.

It was much later when his heart slowed down, and he was hard again, Bridget's face firmly planted in his thoughts. This was going to be a long, long night.

* * *

Come Thursday night, Bridget stared at her reflection in the mirror. A movie date . . .

She laughed out loud.

Pepsi meowed in response.

Glancing over her shoulder, she smiled. "I can't believe I'm going to the movies with Chad Gamble."

The cat cocked its head. Shell had the same response during lunch when Bridget had told her that going to the movies with Chad wasn't that big of a deal. Apparently everything with the ball player was a big deal.

Bridget turned back to the mirror and tucked her hair behind her ears. The distressed blue jeans and red sweater seemed casual enough for a movie date. Sticking her leg out, she turned her ankle. Her heels were red, blue, black, and yellow. Striped. Awesome.

Straightening the hem on her sweater, she turned. The roses sat beside her bed. She hadn't planned on bringing them home yesterday, but she couldn't leave them in the office. Her ex had sent her flowers once, and they'd been the kind that came in a box. Somewhere between the card, the text messages, and tonight, Bridget decided she should at least enjoy some of the advantages of having a pretend boyfriend, especially the three *F*s.

Flowers. Fine dining. Fine-looking man.

And threw in an *N*: No expectations.

The whole blackmail aspect was terrible and still irked the hell out of Bridget, but she wasn't the type of person to continuously dwell on the negative. She had her bitchy moments that lasted a couple of days. She had a right to be ticked off, but this was the hand she was dealt. Though spending the next month mouthing off to Chad might be entertaining for the masses, it wasn't particularly fun for her.

So she might as well enjoy it because a part of her *did* like hanging out with him. When they'd been in the club, they'd really clicked. All she had to do was keep her head in the game. Don't read into anything and most of all do not fall for him. And to keep that from happening, all she had to do was remember the three girls in the paper he'd slept with a few days after they met at the club.

And when was the last time she went to the movies with a guy? Too long.

On the way out, she stopped by Pepsi and scratched him under the chin and then placed a quick kiss on his furry little head. She grabbed her bag and rushed down her apartment steps before he got there. She didn't want him to be in her apartment. The place was her sanctuary and that was entirely too intimate for them.

Chad in her place was a line she wasn't going to cross.

As she hit the front lobby door, she saw Todd Newton. It was strange seeing him wearing more than boxers.

He smiled when he saw her and caught the door, holding it open. "Hey, Miss Rodgers . . ."

Bridget grinned. "Hi, Todd."

His gaze dipped. "You're looking good."

Considering their conversations had always been limited to seeing each other across the hall, this was the first time they were within breathing distance. Up close, she noticed Todd's hazel eyes were more green than brown.

He's really good-looking, she realized. "Thanks. Same goes for you."

Todd's smile spread. He didn't have dimples like Chad, but it was still a great smile. "You heading out?" he asked.

Before Bridget could respond, a deep male voice cut in. "Yes. She's going out with me."

Her heart flopped over heavily. She hadn't seen Chad approach, but there he was, standing right behind Todd with a dark look on his face.

Todd twisted at the waist and then took a surprised step back. Was it possible Todd was the only person in DC who wasn't up to date on Chad's love life?

He extended a hand. "Chad Gamble? Wow. Nice to meet you."

Chad didn't smile, but he took the other man's hand. His eyes were a deep blue and his stare territorial and possessive. A shiver went down her spine. No way she'd admit to liking it. He echoed Todd's sentiment, although Bridget highly doubted he meant a word. "Nice to meet you."

Todd dropped Chad's hand and glanced back to where Bridget stood. "You're a lucky man, Chad, in more ways than one."

Bridget's brows shot up.

A tight smile appeared on Chad's face as he took Bridget's boneless hand. "That I know. Have a nice evening."

Bridget let Chad drag her around the corner of her apartment building toward where his Jeep was illegally parked along the curb. She was surprised it still had its wheels.

"Is that why you didn't want me to meet you at your apartment?" Chad asked as he opened the passenger car door for her.

Her brows knitted in confusion. "Huh?"

"Seems like that guy was really happy about running into you outside." Still at the side of the Jeep, he reached in once she was seated and tugged the seat belt around.

"I can buckle myself in."

"Hey, I'm big on safety. Who was that guy?"

Bridget pulled her hands back with a sigh. "He's just someone who lives across the hall from me. I'm pretty sure that's the longest conversation I've ever had with him."

"Really?" The back of his knuckles brushed the swell of her breasts as he brought the strap over, causing her to suck in a sharp gasp. His gaze lifted, eyes flaring sapphires. A half smile appeared on his lips as he buckled her in. "The guy seems like a dork."

A surprised laugh escaped her. "You don't even know him."

"Neither do you." He flashed a quick smile. "So for all you know, he definitely could be a dork."

Shaking her head, she watched him shut the door and head around the front. Was Chad jealous? No. That didn't make any sense. Boyfriends got jealous, which wasn't what he really was, and he didn't seem like the kind of guy who would ever get jealous.

When they pulled out into traffic, she glanced at him sideways. "So . . . thank you for the flowers. They were really beautiful."

That little lopsided grin remained. "Beautiful flowers for a beautiful woman."

She opened her mouth to point out that was pretty cheesy, but she was trying a more diplomatic approach to this setup and that wouldn't help. "Did you have a good day?" A look of surprise crossed his striking face, and she couldn't help but smile. "What?"

He ran a hand through his hair and gave his head a little shake. "Oh, it's nothing. I just didn't think you'd be interested."

Bridget frowned and was about to ask why he'd think that, but then it struck her. They were pretending, which would mean in reality she shouldn't care about his day. It was like talking on the phone at work, opening up the conversation with general BS and then getting right to the point of the call. This was just a job to him. Maybe Chad didn't want to do anything other than put a show on when the cameras were snapping. The sour feeling in the back of her throat had nothing to do with disappointment. Must've been indigestion.

As Chad navigated the back-to-back traffic, he cleared his throat. "Nothing really happened today. Started with my off-season trainer and that took up all the morning. Then I checked in with Miss Gore." At Bridget's sudden scowl, he chuckled deeply. "Yeah, that was about as fun as playing chicken with a Mack truck. She thought she needed to tell me that I should buy popcorn and soda at the movies. Then I pretty much sat around the bulk of the day. Fun stuff. How about you?"

Bridget fidgeted with the strap on her purse. "Thankfully I didn't have to talk to Miss Gore."

He nodded. "You really don't like that woman, do you?"

"Nope," she replied. "I spent most of the day tracking down the caterer for the fund-raising Gala."

"That's the big one the Smithsonian hosts every year?"

Surprised that he knew anything about it, she nodded. His gaze flicked over to her before returning to the road. "Maddie's talked about it before. You guys have been working on it for a while, right?"

"Yep, all year it feels like. And it's funny we spend this much time on an event that's over in a couple of hours."

"Kind of like Christmas, eh? Months and months of everyone preparing for it, and it's over in a few hours."

"Yeah, like Christmas," she said, turning her gaze to the window.

There was a pause. "Not a fan of Christmas?"

Bridget shook her head.

As if sensing that was a topic she didn't want to go into, he swiftly got the subject back on track. "So when is the Gala?"

"January the second." She wetted her lips. "We've discovered that people tend to be more giving in the New Year. And we need a lot of money or . . ."

"Or what?"

She bit down on her lip. "Or Madison could lose the funding after third quarter next year."

"Really? Shit." He took the curve up ahead and immediately had to brake as there was a line of people turning into the parking garage serving the theatre. "How much money do you guys have to raise?"

"A lot?" she said, letting out a little laugh. "We needed to hit close to five mil and we're about a million short."

"Whoa—that's a lot, but you guys probably have some donors with deep pockets, right?"

"We do, but we've maxed most of them out. So we're shooting for a Hail Mary with this."

They'd finally slid into a parking space and Chad killed the engine, facing her. "What happens if you guys lose your funding?"

Bridget unbuckled herself when it was evident Chad trusted her to do that all by herself. "There'll be a lot of cutbacks. Madison will be fine."

His dark brows furrowed. "I know Maddie will be fine. If she lost her job due to cutbacks, she has Chase. What about you?"

She reached for the door. "They'd probably get rid of my position. I'd either be sucked into another department, or I'll be let go."

"What?"

"Yeah, look, this is really kind of a sucky conversation. I'm sure everything's going to be fine and we're going to be late to the movie." Bridget forced a smile she really wasn't feeling. If Chad thought the fact that she could lose her job was terrible, then he'd probably be horrified by how much in debt she was. "And your adoring public is awaiting you."

Tension pulled at the corners of his lips, but he nodded. She met him around the side of his car, and he took her hand like she expected. For a moment, they both stood there and stared at each other.

The lopsided grin appeared once more. "You do look very nice tonight."

Her lips pursed. "Just jeans and a sweater—nothing amazing."

"They look good on you."

Feeling her cheeks heat, she looked away. The simple compliment that was probably meant to put her at ease shouldn't have gotten her heart racing, but it did. "Flattery will get you nowhere," she said.

"Damn. There goes my master plan to get you in bed just by saying you look nice."

She cracked a grin.

"Come on," he said, tugging her toward the entrance. Just as they reached the double doors, yellow light spilled from inside the building onto the dark sidewalk. His cell phone went off. Reaching into his front pocket with his free hand, he pulled it out and snorted.

"What?" she asked, nervous about heading into the crowded lobby.

Chad laughed. "It's from Miss Gore."

"Goody."

Shaking his head, he slipped his phone back in his pocket. "She wanted to make sure I was holding your hand."

Bridget laughed. "Aw, she's like your mommy giving you pointers."

After opening the door for them, he arched a brow at her as he led her in, and she laughed. A smile formed on his lips in response. As soon as he turned, facing those in line for buying tickets, the double takes started. It was almost comical—one head turning right after the other.

The purchase of tickets was rather uneventful, but as they waited in line to buy popcorn and drinks, because God help them if they let Miss Gore down, the whispers rose like a wave and the stares grew pointed.

Bridget shifted her weight from one foot to the next and kept her gaze leveled on the glass counter ahead. The tips of her ears felt hot.

"Large popcorn with extra butter and salt and . . ." Chase paused. "A cherry soda, right?"

"Perfect."

"Make that two cherry sodas, then."

As they waited, Chase let go of her hand and slipped his arm around her shoulders. Turning so that his body blocked most of hers, he bent his head and whispered, "They'll get bored with us soon enough."

Grateful he was blocking most of the stare-mongers and even a few who were snapping pics on their phones, she turned her face toward his chest. God, he smelled great. Spice and pure male.

Once they got their popcorn and headed toward some action movie, they were stopped for an autograph. Chad handled it gracefully and then there was another autograph. She thought they might get mobbed inside the room but was shocked to discover that hardly anyone was at the showing.

Chad stopped at the back row, letting her squeeze past him. She picked a seat in the middle and sat, helping him with the sodas.

The previews—her favorite part of going to the movies—started seconds later, but as soon as the movie started and stuff was blowing up left and right, her attention wandered . . . right to the man sitting beside her.

He was watching the movie—at least that's what it looked like to her. In the shadowy theatre, his profile was starkly defined, really a work of art. There was no wonder he was voted sexiest man alive.

Tight coils sprung in her belly as her gaze drifted over his cheekbones and lips. His shoulders were wide—

"You're staring at me," he said gruffly.

"No. I'm not." She popped a kernel into her mouth. "Your imagination."

He cast a sidelong glance her way. "Terrible liar."

"You're not watching the movie, either," she pointed out and snuck another handful of popcorn.

His lips curled up on one corner as he leaned over so his arm was pressed against hers. Lowering his head to her ear, he moved the popcorn to her lap. "Well, there is something more interesting going on."

Bridget turned to him and gasped when her lips brushed his chin. Neither of them moved for a few seconds, and then his lips were on hers. No other warning. The kiss was long and deep.

"You taste like butter," he groaned against her lips, and she flushed. "I like it."

She placed a hand on his chest, to push him away or pull him forward she wasn't sure, but then he kissed her once more. Her body—her entire being—was so caught up in the way his lips tasted her and how his hand gripped her shoulder, his fingers flexing like he wanted to move them elsewhere but didn't, and damn if she didn't want to arch her back, showing him just exactly where she wanted him to touch her.

This was insane.

When he pulled back, his eyes searched her face for something.

"We shouldn't be doing that kind of stuff," she whispered, dazed. "No one is looking . . ."

His eyes were latched onto hers. "I know, but I wanted to

and I pretty much do what I want." Smiling, he turned back to the screen. Someone was chasing someone. "This is a damn good movie."

"Yeah," she breathed unsteadily. "It's a very good movie."

But what was going to happen when the movie ended . . . ? Bridget shivered, seriously doubting her self-control for the umpteenth time that night.

Chapter Fourteen

Saturday night was supposed to be like a slumber party. Not that Chad had ever had a slumber party in his entire life, since the last time he checked in his pants he was a dude. But that's what Miss Gore said tonight would be like.

They did a late dinner at Tony's and Tony's, an Italian-style restaurant Bridget had been convinced was run by the mob. That made Chad laugh before he'd accused her of her Irish blood showing through.

The dinner was good. After a little while, Bridget relaxed and she seemed to be handling the attention a bit better, but every time someone would approach their table, she would grow very still or dip her chin forward, using her hair to shield her face.

He couldn't figure that out. Bridget was a total babe. Guys were checking her out when they came in the restaurant. One guy was staring at her like she was the finest piece of steak, and that hadn't made Chad all happy, happy, joy, joy, either.

Which was really strange, he realized as he took care of the check. Normally, he didn't give two shits about guys checking out his dates.

"Thanks," he said, handing over the signed check to the waiter. "You ready?"

Bridget picked up her clutch and stood, and hot damn, he wasn't a big fan of the turtleneck thing she had going on, but he loved how the skirt clung to her legs, and those peek-aboo-fuck-me heels were all right in his book, too.

They were going back to his place.

Bridget was going to stay the night.

Tonight was going to be a very, very long night.

"Do you think people are waiting outside?" she asked as they neared the front door.

"Ah . . ." He stretched up to see beyond some dumbass bronze wall. A light snow fell outside, blanketing the sidewalk. Waiting on the curb were two men huddled down in their jackets, cigarettes in hand and cameras around their necks. Speaking of jackets . . .

Chad looked down at Bridget and frowned. "Where is your jacket?"

She shrugged. "I don't like them."

"It's snowing outside."

"Is it?" Her eyes popped wide as she craned her neck. Glee lit up her face. "Oh! It is! I love the snow."

But not Christmas, apparently, he thought. "You should be wearing a jacket."

"You're not," she pointed out as he led her around the bronze wall and past a group of businessmen who looked like they were seconds away from pouncing on Chad.

"I'm a guy."

Her answering huff brought a grin to his face. Outside, he pulled her under his arm and tucked her close while the valet got the car. Of course it was just because of the snow and she had to be cold and there were the picture people, snapping away, and no other reason than that. Excuses. Excuses.

"Hey, Chad!" one of the photographers called out.

He turned at the waist, recognizing the young guy who usually covered the games. "What's up, Morgan? You're a little far from the stadium, aren't you?"

Morgan grinned as he swaggered closer, his gaze moving to Bridget and then darting back to Chad, but not fast enough that Chad missed it. "Nothing's going on tonight, so they got me stalking you."

"Made your life, didn't it?" Chad could practically hear Bridget's eyes roll.

"You're a big deal." Morgan glanced at Bridget again. Snow dotted her hair and cheeks like a transparent veil. Morgan extended his hand to her. "I'm Morgan—Chad's favorite photographer."

Bridget smiled and shook his hand. "I didn't know he had favorites."

"He's just shy about his affections, especially when it comes to talking about you. Everyone is dying to get your name."

She glanced up at Chad and then took a deep breath. "Bridget Rodgers. Pleasure to meet Chad's favorite stalker."

Morgan laughed, and Chad knew Morgan was filing that name away by the look of eagerness on the photo-hag's face. Luckily, before more questions could be asked, the valet showed up and Chad got Bridget in the Jeep. He blasted the heat as she ran her hands through her hair and back from her face as she smoothed the tiny snowflakes out of her hair. The motion arched her back, thrusting her chest out. The front of her sweater stretched, and it was a damn good thing he wasn't driving yet because he was like a sixteen-year-old-boy and—

"There's no turning back now," Bridget said, lowering her arms. She looked at him. "Right?"

Chad dragged his gaze to her face. Yeah, there was no turning back.

"Now that they know my name?" she added, brows arched. "There's no turning back."

Oh. Yeah. Right. She wasn't talking about her and him, heading back to his place. Chad nodded. "No. There's probably no turning back."

As he pulled into traffic, Bridget twisted in her seat. They went about a block and her brows furrowed as she faced the front. "Are we being followed?"

His gaze flicked to the rearview mirror. A dark Suburban that had been parked along the curb at Tony's and Tony's was right behind them. "It's not Morgan. Probably the guy who was outside with him."

"Man, Miss Gore really knows her stuff."

It was why Bridget was staying the night and would be for at least three more weekends. "If they can get pictures of you going into my place and leaving in the morning, then it's the real deal."

Distaste pulled at her full lips. "Are you okay with this?"

"Hmm?"

"Okay with people following you around all the time?

Knowing when you have people staying over and stuff like that?" she elaborated. "You have an army of stalkers."

"I don't know. Warmed up?" When she nodded, he hit the down arrow on the thermostat. "I really don't think about it."

She appeared to consider that. "Because you're used to it?"

Chad nodded. "I guess you can say that."

"Well, you've been playing ball since you were twenty, right? That's ten years of this, so I guess you would be." She paused, and he was surprised that she knew when he'd started playing ball. Had to be Maddie. "Still seems like a total violation of privacy."

"Comes along with the job, though."

Bridget didn't respond to that and a companionable silence lasted until he pulled into the parking garage. They swung by her car to grab her overnight bag. Of course, the thing was the size of a small van and featured a kaleidoscope of colors.

"Bag?" he asked, offering his hand.

"Why?"

He smiled. "Trying out the gentleman thing and was going to carry it for you."

"There're no cameras around." Then she lowered her voice. "Are there? Oh my God, are they inside?"

"Just give me the bag."

Bridget handed it over, and he steered them toward the door. "No one is inside. The security won't let them into the garage or the doors downstairs."

She followed him into his building and down the empty

hall. Once inside his toasty apartment, he dropped his keys on the counter and then dug out his cell, leaving it there.

"Which guest bedroom do you want?" he asked. "There's one downstairs, but the bathroom is out in the hall. The two upstairs have their—"

"I remember," she said, eyeing the stairs. "I'll take the bedroom downstairs."

"Suit yourself." He carried her bag over to the door under the stairs and nudged it open with his hip. The room was really bare. Just a bedside table, a bed with two pillows and a thin cover, and a small TV mounted to the wall.

"I like the walls," she said, following him in.

Chad smiled to himself. It was the only thing with color—red walls. "I'll get you a heavier blanket. I turn the heat down at night," he offered as an explanation. He put the bag on the bed and shoved his hands into his jeans. "You can also order any movies you want."

She looked around, her gaze dropping to the hardwood floors. "Is this what you do when you normally bring women back to your place?"

Hell no. Usually he took them straight to one of the guest rooms—never his—or they didn't even make it that far. Bridget had been the first woman he'd taken to his bedroom, and he hadn't even realized that until now.

"No, Bridget, this isn't what I normally do. You should remember what I normally do."

She let out a soft, low laugh that had his stomach muscles clenching. "This is so awkward."

Chad stared at her a moment, his gaze soaking up the deep red of her hair, the delicate arches of her cheekbones, and the lush swell of her breasts. He forced himself to look away before he took her to the floor and buried himself in her so deeply that he wouldn't know where he ended and she began. "Want a drink?"

"Yeah, that would be great."

They went back into the kitchen, and he opened the cabinet where he stored the drinks. "Your choice."

Bridget peered over his shoulder. "I better stick with wine. Something sweet, if you have it."

He found some bubbly champagne that Maddie had given him but he'd never drunk. While he poured her a glass and got a little scotch out for himself, he watched her wander aimlessly through the kitchen and into the living room once she had her drink.

Chad took a few moments in the kitchen to himself. Closing his eyes, he swore under his breath. All night he'd been fighting the urge to crush his mouth and his body to hers. He strolled into the living room and checked out the window. A wry grin pulled at his lips. "We've got company."

She came to his side, and he inhaled her jasmine scent. "Is that the Suburban that was following us?"

"Yep."

"And he's going to sit out there all night?"

"Yep."

She backed away from the window, eyes narrowed as she took a sip of her champagne. "You've been through this a lot, haven't you? With other women you were . . . well, you weren't pretending with?"

Chad turned from the window. "Not to sound repetitive, but yep."

Sitting down on the leather couch, she kicked off her heels and tucked her feet under her. A weird feeling occurred in his chest, followed by the even more bizarre thought that she looked good sitting there on his couch. Like that made any fucking sense.

A couple of moments passed and then she asked, "Do you really think this is going to work?"

Walking over to Bridget, he sat on the ottoman in front of her. "I don't know." He shrugged, taking a drink. "Miss Gore seems to know her shit. I haven't gotten any angry calls from my manager in a few days."

A small smile appeared. "But what about afterward? It's really going to be . . ."

"Me changing my ways?" he supplied, and then he laughed. "Yeah, I have to cut back on the partying."

Bridget watched him through those soulful green eyes. "And the women?"

"The women aren't as many as people think they are."

"Uh huh," she murmured. "Can I ask you a question?"

Leaning forward, he nodded. "Shoot."

"If you know that you have these photographers following you around and people are constantly snapping photos of you while you're out, why do you do the things you do? You have to know it's going to be all over the papers."

The glass dangled from his fingertips. "And should I live my life differently because of that? Is that fair?"

"You shouldn't have to live your life differently." Her pink tongue darted out, wetting her lips, and his body jumped to attention. "But is it necessary to be doing it with three ladies at once?"

So caught up in staring at her lips, what she said didn't process immediately. "I didn't sleep with three ladies at once. Okay. Wait. Not anytime recently."

Doubt clouded her eyes. "Okay."

"I'm being serious." He sat up straight. "I didn't do anything with those women other than make a dumbass decision of jumping in bed with them. Clothes stayed on. No kissing or touching. I was in that bed for about thirty seconds, enough time for someone to snap a picture."

Bridget stared at him for so long he wondered if she'd been struck silent, and then she lowered her gaze to her drink. "What about the model you were pictured with?"

He'd been pictured with a lot of models over the years.

"Stella," she said, throwing him a bone. "What about her?"

"Stella?" He laughed. "We did some things a long time ago, but we're just friends now. When she comes into town, we hang out at a bar or with friends. Sometimes she stays here in one of the guest rooms."

Bridget's cheeks were a little flushed as she put her empty glass down on the end table. "How long ago is a 'long time ago' in your world?"

Chad debated not answering, suddenly unsure if his "long time ago" was going to be long enough for whatever Bridget was thinking. "Almost a year ago. You'd like her. You guys have the same kind of fashion thing going on."

Her brows rose in a way that said, *Doubtful.*

"Refill?" When she nodded, he did the waiter thing and returned to the ottoman. "Any other questions you want to ask?"

A sexy little smirk appeared on her lips. "Yes. I do."

Chad chuckled. "Okay, but if you ask me a question, I get to ask you one."

After taking a drink, she leaned back against the supple cushions and arched a brow. "Okay. Deal."

Shaking the ice in his scotch, he mirrored her expression. "Go ahead."

"When's the last time you've had sex?"

Chad let out a short laugh. "Wow. You go right for the big stuff, don't you?" He liked the way her cheeks flamed. "Okay. It's been several months."

Bridget snickered. "Whatever."

His brows slammed down as he leaned forward and tapped a finger on her knee. "I'm not lying."

"You?" She laughed. "You haven't had sex in a couple of months."

"No. Going on three-and-a-half months to be exact."

"Oh. Record-breaker." Her wide smile slipped off her lips the longer he stared at her. "Hell. You're being serious?"

He took a drink and nodded. "Serious as a massive heart attack."

"Cornball," she said. "Three months isn't a long time, but that's impressive for you."

"Geez, thanks." But Chad wasn't insulted. He liked sex. A lot. And did it. A lot. He was always careful, used protection, and operated the "If he was too drunk to walk, he was too drunk to fuck" rule that went for all parties involved. "How about you? How long has it been since you had sex?"

Bridget eyed him through thick lashes. "Longer than three months."

"How long?" Damn. He really needed to know.

She didn't answer him immediately, instead taking another drink. "It's going on two years."

Chad schooled his expression. "Two years . . . ?"

"Go ahead." She waved a hand. "Say something smartass."

"Wasn't planning on it," he said, his gaze dropping to her lips again. "So are we talking no sexual interaction for two years or just no sex?"

She unfolded her legs, causing her knee to brush his. "It's my turn. Do you regret leaving college for baseball?"

Again, he was a little surprised by how much she knew, but considering how much Maddie liked to talk, he shouldn't be so shocked. "Yes and no. If I blow out my arm, it would be nice to have a different kind of career to fall back on, but I could always work with one of my brothers."

"Which one?" she asked.

He *tsk*ed and gently nudged her knee with his. "My turn. Are we talking no sexual interaction or no sex?"

Her eyes rolled. "Nothing up until the night I went home with you."

Oh yeah, he was really liking the sound of that. "And after?"

"Answer my question." She set her half-finished drink aside.

Chad grinned. "I'd probably do something with Chandler. His job's a bit unorthodox, but it would at least be interesting."

Bridget bit down on her lip. "I could see you doing that—the bodyguard thing. And no."

"What are you saying no to?"

Her cheeks turned pink. "Nothing before or after you. Happy?"

Chad's eyes met hers. "Yes. Very happy."

Chapter Fifteen

She didn't look away or giggle or lower her lashes or do any number of flirty behaviors. Their eyes locked, and he saw what he had the night in the club and in his bedroom. Heat. Need. Want. His state of arousal amplified to a million. Confined by his jeans, his cock swelled to an almost painful state.

God, he wanted nothing more than to get on his knees and pay worship to her.

Bridget's chest rose sharply, and finally she broke eye contact. Reaching for her glass, she nearly downed the whole thing . . . and that was kind of hot. "So . . ." She cleared her throat. "Madison never told me what you studied in college."

"Sports management," he answered, voice husky. "You?"

"History." She smiled a little.

"History nerd?"

"You betcha."

They went back and forth like that, taking turns asking one question after another. At some point, he moved to sit beside her, their legs pressed together. Hours passed. Another glass was refilled. He discovered she had wanted to be an anthropologist but had decided not to go that route. She didn't elaborate, and when he told her that his parents had never watched one of his games, she didn't push it. She talked about the Gala and he told her what it was like to live on the road during the season. Every so often, their eyes would meet and that unspoken yearning burned alive.

She wanted him—that much he knew. Maybe even as much as he wanted her, and his body was strung tight, his cock throbbing each time she shifted and their bodies brushed.

But as it neared one a.m. and she stood to go to bed, he let her. He actually fucking stood there and said good night.

Bridget stopped under the stairwell, her hair a deep auburn in the soft light. "Good night, Chad."

He felt himself nod and then forced one foot in front of the other, going not where his body so wanted to go. Inside his bedroom, he closed the door behind him and then leaned against it, pressing his forehead against the cool wood. "Shit."

Tonight really *was* going to be the longest night of his life, especially since self-restraint wasn't something he typically practiced.

Bridget considered going naked. The pajama bottoms and tank top felt like too much on her hypersensitive skin. She was too old and too realistic to blame the champagne on the glow she was rocking right now or her ultra-bright eyes staring back from the bathroom mirror outside the guest room.

It was due to one hundred percent Grade-A Chad.

With her ex, she'd never been this turned on. So ready for sex that every time she moved and her clothes brushed against her skin, she wanted to cry.

Hell, the one person who had ever left her body burning without even touching her had been Chad. She wasn't sure she could do this, stay the night knowing he was only feet away.

After yanking her toothbrush out of her toiletry bag, she squirted toothpaste on it and set about brushing her teeth with a little too much vigor. When she finished, she turned off the water and clenched the toothbrush as she stared at her reflection.

"I like the jammies."

Chad filled the doorway to the bathroom, startling her. His bare feet peeked out from underneath the hem of jeans that hung so low on his hips she wondered if he was wearing anything underneath them. He'd lost the shirt and sweater and his rock-hard abs were on full display.

Good God . . .

It looked like someone had placed indentations next to his hips, and she wanted to lick those chiseled slopes and then move on to each hard ripple. The man had a body to worship.

Heart pounding, she put her toothbrush back into its bag. When she was sure she was breathing normally, she faced him completely. "I thought you were going to bed."

His stare was heavy-lidded. "I'm not tired."

She gripped the edge of the sink with one hand as her chest rose and fell rapidly. His gaze dipped and through the thinned slits, his eyes were a deep, intense blue. Under his concentrated stare, her nipples hardened and the low fire that had been simmering all night long rushed through her veins. There was no mistaking her arousal. The tank was thin.

Bridget's brain just clicked off and her body took over. Pulse thrumming, she felt no need to cover herself. "I'm not tired, either."

Chad was on her in an instant.

Her gasp was cut off as he wrapped one powerful arm around her waist and pulled her against him. With her front against his, there was no questioning his desire or what he wanted, either. She felt his long and thick arousal pressed against her belly and her knees went weak. She gripped his shoulders, his skin hot and firm.

This was insane. "We shouldn't be doing this."

One hand tightened on her hip and the other traveled up her spine, leaving delicious shivers in its wake. "Probably not," he admitted.

Good to know they were on the same page, but she didn't pull away and neither did he. That traveling hand of his delved deep into her hair and cradled the nape of her neck. Her breath came out in short bursts.

"Chad . . ." She trailed off as the hand on her hip skated down, cupping her rear. Heat exploded through her core.

His lips were a hairsbreadth from hers, tantalizingly close. "Yeah, we shouldn't be doing this." His voice was a low growl. "But can you tell me you don't want this?"

Bridget knew she should, but the words wouldn't come out of her mouth. She couldn't look away from the intensity of his gaze.

"Didn't think so," he said, and lowered his head. His lips brushed against her lower one, and her hands tightened on his shoulders. "You want this as badly as I do." To punctuate his words, he moved against her, and she bit back a moan. "Isn't that right, Bridget?"

Oh, she did.

Chad made another slow, teasing sweep against her mouth. "Admit it."

The hand on her ass tightened, and then he lifted her onto the tips of her toes so that his arousal pressed into her core. Her eyes drifted shut and her mouth opened. When he kissed her, his tongue slid over hers and then across the roof of her mouth, and she moaned softly.

"Admit it," he said against her lips.

She shook her head.

He smiled and slipped his hand away from her neck, down to her aching breast. At first, his hand just skimmed over the swell, eliciting a muffled whimper from her. Then his thumb found the hardened peak and teased the nub until he was breathing as heavily as she was.

"I want to hear you say it, Bridget." His thumb and forefinger pinched her nipple, and she cried out. A smug, satisfied grin split his lips. "Bridget?"

She clamped her mouth shut.

Challenge flared in Chad's eyes. Letting go of her rear, he let her slide down and then both hands were on her breasts. Lowering his head, he caught the other peak in his mouth and suckled through the thin cotton. She cried out as pleasure rolled through her.

"Say it," he teased, biting down gently.

Bridget could barely think around what he was doing. His fingers teased one nipple as his mouth tortured the other. He backed her up, until she was pressed against the glass shower door. The coolness against her back and the hotness on her front sent her mind spinning.

As he sucked harder, he slid a hand down her belly and over the flare of her hip, then to her front. He slipped his hand between her thighs, his fingers moving down the seam of her pajamas, creating a wild friction. Her hips rolled against the movement as she pressed her head back. She went wet between her legs, so close to release already she was sure her heart was going to explode in her chest. Her body shuddered.

Then Chad let go, taking a step away from her. His hands closed into fists at his sides as he stood before her, and she could see the length of his arousal pushing against his jeans. He stared at her like a man on the verge of losing all control.

"Say it, Bridget, or God help me . . ."

A wicked thrill went through her. "Yes."

"Yes to what, Bridget?" The deepness in his voice stroked her.

An unbearable heat built. "Yes. I want you."

Bridget had never seen a man move so fast. His arms were around her, his lips demanding and ravishing. Chad spun her around and they were moving backward, out of the bathroom, his mouth never leaving hers. His hands were everywhere, on her hips, her breasts, sliding between her thighs.

They didn't make it to the bedroom.

When the back of her legs hit the couch, he hooked his

fingers under the hem of her tank top. Not giving her much of a chance to feel self-conscious, he tugged the material up and over.

Standing back at arm's length, she saw the muscles in his shoulders and chest bulge and tense, taking her breath away. "You're so beautiful," he said in a way that made it sound like a prayer of sorts.

Her heart fluttered crazily as she stood before him, letting him take his fill of her. A flush stole down her neck and traveled farther south. She'd never stood like this before, letting a man soak her in. She felt intensely vulnerable, and in the same respect, deeply powerful.

Chad moved forward and when he placed a hand on her cheek, she swore it trembled. "So fucking beautiful," he said again, kissing her gently.

"Thank you," she whispered.

He smiled, and his hands settled on her shoulders, pushing her down until she was on her back and he was kneeling over her. Then his lips were on the swell of her breasts. As he laved and suckled, his other hand slipped between her legs to her core. She pressed against his palm as she skated her fingertips down the hard planes of his chest and his stomach, and then lower.

His growl of approval brought a smile to her lips. Then he was tugging her bottoms down and she lifted up, aiding in the process. Their eyes met and air punched out of her lungs.

There was definitely no going back from this, as wrong or crazy as it may be.

Chad's hard thigh parted hers, and then he was cupping

her. A finger slid inside her slick folds, setting up a mind-blowing rhythm as his mouth captured her soft cries.

Unlike last time, she *was* going to touch him.

Bridget tugged his jeans down his legs and his hard, hot length landed on her thigh. Good Lord, he was big—bigger than she expected. She wrapped her hand around the base of him and he stilled, his finger deep inside her.

"Bridget," he ground out. "If you touch me, I'm not going to last. I want you too badly to play around."

His words hummed in her blood, melting her into a pool of heat. She wanted him to lose control, to prove just how affected he was by her. Bridget's hand slid down the smooth length of him, and she loved how his body jerked at her touch. She did it again, and he rewarded her by slipping another finger deep inside her. Her thumb smoothed over the head and his tongue speared her mouth. They moved against each other, their hips straining. A tremble ran through Chad, transferring to her. Every muscle locked up. Chad's movements picked up pace, his fingers going in and out of her as she moved her hand over his pulsing sex.

When he pressed down on the bundle of nerves, her world tilted and then blew apart. His kisses caught the sound of her release as she shattered, her body spasming against him and her hand tightening on his sex. Chad let out a ragged groan as he punched his hips in her hand. As aftershocks rocked her core and her entire being, Chad came with a roar, his big, hard body shaking against her softer one.

As he settled down, she tentatively moved her other hand to his bent head, running her fingers through his hair. He turned into the touch, tilting his head to the side. Dark lashes framed his cheekbones as she stroked him. They stayed like that for several heartbeats, and then he opened his eyes.

"I'm not done with you," he said. "Not yet. Not until I'm deep inside you."

She felt him thicken and harden against her belly, and a shudder rocked her. Oh yeah, she liked the sound of that. Her body was primed and so, so ready.

Chad prowled over to her, and she felt good caged in between those powerful arms, but when he kissed her flushed forehead and then the tip of her nose, she lost a little of herself forever. The sweet gesture swept through her, and she squeezed her eyes shut against the sudden rush of tears.

There was nothing sexy about what he just did, not sexy in the way it was all about two bodies coming together with one goal in mind. The act was something lovers did, and her heart swelled so fast she was afraid she was going to say something stupid and horrifying.

They wanted each other—yes. There was a mutual, powerful attraction between them—yes. He was going to bring her pleasure she had never imagined—yes. But none of that changed the fact that they were pretending to date. There were no feelings. No future. All made worse by the fact that Chad could be incredibly charming.

But having sex with him, forming that kind of intimate bond, was going to be so much harder to break and get over when this month ended and she never saw him again.

Bridget had gotten her heart broken before, and she really didn't want to experience that crushing weight again—not with someone like Chad, whom she doubted she could easily recover from.

For the second time, she put the brakes on what was happening between them.

Putting her hands on his shoulders, she pushed. It wasn't a hard push, but he stilled and stared down at her with eyes the color of the deepest, clearest oceans. "What?"

She took a stuttered breath. "I think . . . I think we should stop here."

His eyes searched hers intently, seeking answers she was unwilling to give up easily. "I know you want this."

"I do." Oh God, did she ever. It took all of her effort to keep her body still. "But this is going to just make things complicated, right?" She pulled her hands back and closed them into loose fists in the air between them. "And at the end of December you're going to go your own way and . . . and I'm going to go mine."

Chad stared down at her. For a moment, she thought he might say something about not denying what they both wanted, and oddly she almost wanted him to try to convince her otherwise, to change her mind and . . . *and what*? Work for this? *This* was nothing.

He slid off her and quickly pulled up his jeans. "Yeah, you're right. We wouldn't want to complicate things."

Chapter Sixteen

Over the next two weeks, things progressed as planned. To the public and the Nationals, their relationship was a blossoming love affair of epic proportions. Even Miss Gore was starting to think that something real was going on between them.

"Are you taking her to buy a gown for the Christmas event?" she asked, eyeing him above the rim of her glasses.

Chad pressed the up arrow on the treadmill, hoping to drown out Miss Gore's voice and his own internal annoying-as-hell voice. They'd done the required three dates a week and the stay-over on the weekend, but since the night on the couch, things had been tense. It wasn't that they weren't getting along, because they were. They were getting along "famously," as Miss Gore had put it. Yesterday, he'd taken Bridget to the clubhouse and taught her how to hold a curveball, a change-up, and a fastball. She was ridiculously horrible at positioning her fingers, to the point it was entertaining.

Afterward, they'd had lunch at Hooters down the road with Tony.

Tony liked Bridget, more than Chad appreciated, which

was stupid, because God knew they didn't want to "complicate" things.

Things were already fucking complicated.

Not to mention he was jerking off like he was in damn high school again. Thirty years old, a pro athlete, and richer than sin, and he was jerking off every day instead of getting off in a woman. That's what his life had come down to.

But the even more fucked up thing was that he still could get a piece if he wanted to. Hell, he knew how to be discreet when he chose, but he didn't. He didn't want anyone except the redheaded vixen.

Bridget consumed his thoughts when she was with him or away. For two weeks, he'd been in a constant state of arousal that had only been whetted by what had taken place between them.

"Chad!" snapped Miss Gore. She leaned over the arm of the treadmill and hit the emergency stop button.

At the last minute, he caught himself before he ate the tread. "Jesus!"

"Not quite." She folded her arms. "Have you been listening to me at all?"

"Yes." He grabbed the towel off the front and stepped off the treadmill, mopping up his sweat. "I'm taking her out later today, before dinner, to one of those damn places you picked out that's going to cost me a month's salary."

Miss Gore nodded her approval. "Bridget will like the place."

"How do you know what she likes?" He tore off his shirt and tossed it into a laundry basket. Miss Gore was so not affected by any partial nudity on his end.

She followed him out into the kitchen. "I like her, you know."

Grabbing a bottle of water, he raised a brow at her.

"Your friends seem to like her, too. *You* seem to like her."

Chad downed half of the bottle. "What are you getting at?"

Miss Gore shrugged her bony shoulders. "All I'm saying is that you two are really convincing."

Whatever. He said that out loud, too.

"Well, the good news is that the Nationals are beyond pleased with you." A proud smile tilted the corners of her lips, and she looked almost human for a moment. "The Christmas event they plan should seal the deal. You should be happy about this. There's only a week and some odd days left."

Chad wasn't happy about this.

"Of course, you're not getting rid of me that easily."

Of course not.

"I'll stay on to make sure you maintain your image," she continued. "If we play our cards right, we'll get the public's sympathy after your split from Miss Rodgers."

His eyes narrowed. "Oh, so we're going to make her the villain in all of this?"

"Better than you coming out the bad guy, right?" Miss Gore frowned. "What? Does that bother you?"

Chad didn't say anything, because honestly, what did this woman think of him if she thought he'd be okay with that? There'd be nothing she could say that would get him to let Bridget take the blame. Contract or no.

After a while, Miss Gore left, passing his older brother

Chandler on the way out. The two came to a complete standstill in the foyer. Neither would move out of the way for the other. There couldn't be two more obstinate people in the world, he realized. Chad left them to figure how to enter and exit at the same time.

Later, it turned out Bridget did love the Little Boutique on 27th Avenue. She floated from one rack of sparkly dresses to another while he sat in one of those chairs that reminded him of a throne—a pink throne that someone's grandmother took a Bedazzler to.

Through narrowed eyes, he watched her look over the accessories first. She had her eye on a necklace that appeared to be a real emerald dangling from a silver chain. She kept running her fingers over it, and he thought the stone would match her eyes—

What the hell was he thinking? A necklace would match her eyes? God, he sounded like Chase.

She finally moved over to the dresses, going straight for a deep-green one that looked like it would hug her curves. He hoped she picked that one. His gaze dropped to her sweet, round ass, and he had to look away before things got real awkward up in here.

At the counter, two clerks were giggling and whispering as they stared at him.

Taking a deep breath, he went back to staring at Bridget as he slid farther down in his pink throne, spreading his thighs wide to get a little more comfortable. He saw her pick up the tag and then frown. She dropped the dress.

"Bridget?"

She looked over her shoulder at him. Her hair was pulled

up in a high ponytail and a bright red and purple silk scarf was intricately tied around her neck. "What?"

"I liked that dress." He nodded at the green one she'd held.

Walking over to him, she straightened the edges on the scarf. "I do, too."

"Then try it on."

She bit down on her plump lip, and he was jealous. He wanted to bite it—lick it. "It's too expensive."

He reached into the pocket of his jeans and pulled out a lollipop he'd stolen from the counter when they'd come in. "How much is it?"

"You don't even want to know."

Tearing off the wrapper, he popped the lolli in his mouth. "How much?"

"Too much," she replied.

"How much, Bridget?"

She sighed and her eyes narrowed. "It's a little shy of fifteen hundred."

Chad didn't even blink. "Try it on."

"But—"

"Try it on." When she didn't budge, he arched a brow. "Or I will."

Her stern expression slipped away as she giggled. "Is that supposed to convince me? I'd die to see you in that dress."

Chad swirled the lolli around, eyes narrowing. "I'll try it on right here, in front of the two nice ladies up front. You know, by the counter and the *glass* windows."

"Go ahead," she said, but when he raised both brows, she rolled her eyes and made a sound of disgust. "Fine."

When she spun around, he got an eyeful of the frustrated little twitch in her step and his lips split into a grin. Biting into the hard candy, he watched her stalk past him with the dress in hand, shooting him a dark look.

Of course, the moment he heard the soft *click* of the dressing room door, pictures of her stripping her clothes off filled his head. Images of her wiggling that ass out of those jeans and unhooking her bra, because that dress was strapless, teased him.

Chad shifted in the blitzed-out throne, feeling himself swell.

Twice now Bridget had stopped things right before the real fun could get started. Complicate things? As if the whole situation wasn't already complicated as fuck. So why not just do what they both wanted? Because he knew she wanted him.

As he sat there, the stupidest shit popped into his head. Chad thought about his father. Now that was a man who had pretty much done whatever he wanted, when he wanted. Not that his father's behavior was something to look up to. Hell, the way his father had behaved, as if the world was one giant playground built just for him, had fucked with all their heads. It was why Chase had stayed away from Maddie as long as he had and why Chandler was a controlling, obstinate fuck.

And it was why Chad acted like . . . well, like the world was his playground.

Fuck.

Sitting up straighter, he thought what a fucked-up place to have such a realization. He was sitting in a damn pink throne. And you'd think that would've changed what he was about to do, but it didn't. He was pissed, confused, and horny. Not a good combination.

Chad stood up and tossed the ladies up front a grin and a wink. "I'm going to help her zip her dress."

One of them giggled. "You do that."

Swaggering back down the hall, he knocked on the door and then immediately opened it. The curve of a pale back greeted him. There was a freckle right beside her spine.

Yeah, he was going to get up close and personal with that freckle.

Bridget gasped and jerked around, clutching the front of the green dress to her breasts. Her eyes widened when she saw him. "What are you doing?"

"Remember when I said I was being a good boy? Well, now I'm being naughty."

"Chad!" Her voice came out in a hushed whisper. "We're in a dressing room. There are people right out the—"

"I don't care." He caught her arms, totally not missing the flare of heat in her eyes. Oh, baby, Bridget had a naughty girl in her. "There is something I need to do."

Bridget opened her mouth, probably to ask a shit ton worth of questions, because that woman was inquisitive as hell, but he silenced her words with his mouth. Kissing her, he didn't hold back. He claimed her, forcing her lips open, and just when her body started to tremble, he pulled back and flipped her around, so that her back was against his front.

"We shouldn't be doing this," she said, but her voice was husky and betrayed her needs.

He slid the material down her hips, letting it pool around

her ankles. Then he kissed that freckle and when he licked it, her back arched. He straightened, dragging his hands up her sides. He could see her in the mirror, the rosy tips of her breasts pebbled, begging for him.

Who was he to deny her?

Chad cupped her breasts in both hands from behind and lowered his head, his breath stirring the tiny strands of red hair. "I like the dress."

Bridget's eyes were only half open. "You didn't even see me in it."

"I saw enough to know you'd look good out of the dress." He rolled her nipples between his fingers, causing her to jerk. "So, yeah, I like the dress."

Her breath was coming out in short rasps. "Chad, we need to stop this. This isn't—"

She'd grabbed at his hands, but he easily caught her wrists in one hand. Holding them captured under her breasts, he placed a kiss against her thundering pulse. "This isn't what? Something that you want? Bullshit. You want it."

A shudder rocked her body, and her lashes lowered completely, fanning her flushed cheeks. Chad smiled against her exposed neck as he slid his free hand down her belly, loving the softness of her skin. When his fingers reached the band on her panties, she tried to pull her hands free.

"Oh, no, you're not going anywhere." He kissed the spot below her ear and was rewarded with a shiver. "We're going to do this right now."

In the mirror, he could see her teeth clamped down on her plump lower lip and he knew he had her. "Open your eyes," he ordered. "I want you to watch me."

Bridget's lashes lifted.

"See what I'm doing?" Slipping a hand between her spread thighs, he slid his fingers under the satiny panties. "You like that?"

Heat flared, turning her eyes an emerald shade of green. "Yes," she gasped.

Brushing over her damp folds, he groaned deep in his throat. She was already wet and ready for him.

For. Him.

"Well, you're really going to like this." He eased a finger in her, and it didn't take much.

Bridget's hips immediately rolled into the rhythm, her ass pressing back against his cock over and over, and if he wasn't careful, it was going to be a very awkward walk out of the boutique.

When he felt her muscles starting to tremble, he let go of her wrists and placed his hand over her mouth, silencing her cries. She surprised him, though, when she sucked one of his fingers into her mouth as she came. He felt that all the way to the tip of his dick.

Letting her go when he was sure she wouldn't collapse, he put distance between them. Perhaps this wasn't one of his brightest ideas. The smell of her clung to him, he could still feel her pushing back against him, and now he wanted nothing more than to just take her to the floor. Against the mirror. Fuck, anywhere.

Bridget stared at him, cheeks flushed and eyes glazed, breathing raggedly. "What about you?"

His lips twisted into a smirk. "That'll just complicate things."

"Chad—"

He stopped at the door. "Does the dress fit?"

"Yes, but—"

"Good. We're getting it." He opened the door and pinned her with one last look. Man, if he stared at her any longer, he was going to have her on her knees or on her back. "And don't argue with me about it."

Bridget looked so damn sexy standing there, naked with the exception of her panties and her chin jutting out stubbornly.

Yeah, he needed to get the fuck out of the dressing room now.

Chad dipped out, closing the door behind him. Too bad getting her out of his head wasn't as easy as shutting a door.

Chapter Seventeen

Bridget barely recognized herself in the green dress. The deep hue brought out the matching color in her eyes and flattered her pale complexion and red hair. The material was heavy, concealing any kind of unsightly bulges but didn't feel like she was wearing a curtain.

"You look beautiful," Shell said, putting the finishing touch in Bridget's updo—a silvery clip that held her curls up. "The dress is fantastic."

The dress *was* fantastic. "I can't believe he bought this. Such a wa—"

"If you say waste of money, I will disown you." Shell turned her around and stared at her hard. "It's wonderful that he would do something like this—romantic. You're going to have a wonderful time hanging out with the players and glamorous people."

Bridget swallowed, but her throat was dry. Butterflies were bouncing around her stomach like they were trying to find a way out. She'd met Tony and some of the other guys, but the idea of hobnobbing with all of them made her want to hurl.

"Chad's picking you up from my place?" Shell asked.

She nodded. "Yeah, it's actually closer to his and made sense, since you were doing my hair."

Shell grinned at her. "Gawd girl, you are so damn lucky. I hope you realize that. Chad is a hell of a catch. I'm jealous."

An ache pierced her chest, and she turned back to the mirror, blinking rapidly and hoping she didn't ruin her mascara. This whole thing was almost over. Three days from Christmas and tomorrow was the last day of work for her before the holiday break. Then there was New Year's and the Gala.

Chad probably wouldn't even be around for the Smithsonian event.

According to Miss Gore, the Nationals were thrilled with Chad's improvement. There was no more talk about canceling the contract, and the publicist fully believed that after tonight, his image would be repaired. And what had that evil woman said the last time she'd seen her?

"Chad will probably get the public's sympathy when you guys split," Miss Gore had said. "So this will work out wonderfully."

God, she hated that woman with a passion.

"Bridget?" Shell's voice intruded. "Are you okay?"

Her mouth opened, and she so badly wanted to tell Shell the truth, but how could she? It wasn't like Shell didn't know she'd gotten in trouble over the student loans, but how could she tell anyone that everything that had been between her and Chad had been completely faked?

Except the passion—she was pretty sure that was real.

She forced a smile. "You don't think this dress is too much?"

Shell barked out a short laugh. "Okay. Something is definitely wrong with you if you're asking if any piece of clothing is too much. This is actually pretty tame for you."

It was. With black beading over the heart-shaped bodice, it was nothing like the flamboyant style she usually relied on.

"You look great, Bridget."

"Thank you." Bridget left the bathroom and took a deep breath. "I guess I'm just feeling tired."

Shell nodded. "Well, you better pep up because you need to enjoy yourself. Seriously. You and Chad are like a Cinderella story."

Bridget laughed at that. "I wouldn't go that far."

"Whatever. It's totally—" A knock on her front door cut off her words. She let out a low squeal and spun toward the entrance before Bridget could blink.

Her friend threw open the door. "Helllоooo . . ."

Bridget peered around the corner, and her heart sped up. Her mouth also dropped open. There might have been a little drool.

Chad in a tux was, well, everything any female on the planet could imagine.

His broad shoulders really filled out the jacket in ways most men couldn't. It was a perfect fit, cut to his body and his body alone. With his hair artfully messy and his lips tipped in a half smile, he looked like he stepped right out of a movie or something—right out of a fairy tale.

Chad extended a hand to Shell. "Nice to finally meet you."

She murmured something unintelligible and spun around, mouthing the words *Prince Charming* before spinning back to

Chad. "You're even better looking up close. Most people aren't, but wow, you definitely make the cut."

Bridget grinned.

Taking her friend's outburst good naturedly, Chad laughed. "Well, I'm glad to hear I 'make the cut.'"

As he stepped past her, Shell checked him out from behind. "Yeah, you definitely make the cut."

Okay. That was probably enough. If Bridget didn't intervene, there was a good chance Shell would start touching him. Stepping out into the hall, she gave him a short, awkward wave.

Chad stumbled a little, and Bridget had never seen him stumble. He drew up short and swallowed as his gaze drifted over her. "You look . . . absolutely beautiful."

She felt the blush sweep over her face. "Thank you."

"You both look great." Shell reappeared, holding her phone. "I want a picture."

"This isn't prom, Shell."

Chad chuckled as he held his arm to Bridget. "Come on over here. Let's get our picture taken."

Shooting her friend a look, which was subsequently ignored, Bridget slipped up to Chad's side. His arm went around her waist, and he pulled her closer, tucking her against him.

Shell squealed as she held up the phone. "Smile!"

After a couple of pictures Shell swore wouldn't end up on her Facebook or anywhere else, Bridget and Chad said their good-byes. On the way out, Bridget grabbed the lacy black shawl, and he helped drape it over her shoulders.

"It's pretty chilly outside," he said outside Shell's apartment. "You sure this is enough?"

Bridget nodded.

He smiled slightly. “That’s right. You hate jackets.”

“They’re just so bulky.” Since Shell had a first-floor apartment, it didn’t take long for her to discover just how cold it had become since she’d arrived at her friend’s place.

Outside, she clutched the ends of the shawl together and inhaled deeply. “It smells like—”

“Snow?” he cut in, grinning at her.

Bridget looked at him and felt her heart do that damn little jump again. “Yes. It smells like snow.”

“I heard that it’s calling for snow on Christmas. I can’t remember the last time we had a white Christmas.”

She couldn’t, either. Snow in any real amounts didn’t usually fall until February, and if it was more than an inch, the entire town shut down.

Chad opened the door for her but caught her arm before she could climb in. He leaned in, his lips brushing her temple. “I’m torn,” he said.

“About what?”

His lips curved against her skin. “I can’t decide if you look better in that dress or with it pooled around your ankles.”

Bridget was suddenly hot in the near freezing temperatures. Damn it. She had been trying desperately to forget about those minutes in the dressing room and here he had to bring it up. Liquid fire licked at her, magnified when he placed a hand on her hip.

“Mmm,” he murmured. “I’m going to go with it lying on my bedroom floor.”

Her breath went out in an unsteady rush. "You haven't seen that."

Chad pulled back and there was a cocky grin on his face. "Not yet."

Christmas was everywhere. As they walked into the fancy hotel hosting the event, Bridget was caught up in all the glitz. Garland twisted around the lampposts. Icicle lights hung from the fronts of buildings, glimmering like hundreds of polished diamonds. In the tiny park splitting the congested streets, a decorated Christmas tree glowed brightly.

While Bridget wasn't a huge fan of the holiday, she did love all the shiny things. Most of the year, the city was dull and drab, but come Christmas, the entire town sparkled.

And this hotel was really sparkling.

The Christmas tree in the lobby glimmered gold and silver, so bright and beautiful.

"You like it?" Chad murmured in her ear, placing a hand on her lower back.

She nodded as they stopped in front of the massive tree. "It's beautiful."

"I like the trees that are all different colors. You know, the kind that really doesn't have a theme to them. Maddie's parents have a tree like that, bulbs just thrown up on it. Mismatched tinsel and a star that is *always* crooked."

Bridget smiled. She'd met Madison's parents a few times, and they'd been a riot. She couldn't imagine what Christmas was like at their house. Probably involved decorating bomb shelters and general craziness—the good kind of craziness.

"You know I always do Christmas Eve at their place, right? It's tradition."

Yes. She knew that.

"And this year—"

"I'm not going to Madison's house for Christmas," she said, stepping away from him. "No way is that happening."

His brows puckered. "Do you have plans?"

Did she have plans? She almost laughed. She'd be doing the same thing she did on Christmas for the last nine years. "It's not important. So where's the big party?"

Chad watched her for a moment and then took her hand. "Let's get this show on the road."

Bridget wasn't sure how to prepare herself for this event, but she soon realized nothing could have. They were rushed the moment they stepped into the glittery ballroom.

She was introduced to so many people she couldn't keep their faces straight or remember their names. A glass of champagne was handed to her and then another. Being on the arm of Chad Gamble was really like being with a rock star. It was obvious everyone loved him or at least looked up to him, especially the younger teammates. They were in awe of him.

Pictures were taken, one after another, and she knew a whole boatload of them would be in the newspaper and on the web within hours. When the manager of the Club introduced himself, Bridget glanced at Chad.

Nothing in his expression changed, but he stiffened just the slightest. "How're you doing?" he said, extending his free hand.

"Great. I'm glad to see you here with such beautiful

company." The manager shook Chad's hand and then turned to Bridget. The man's lined face crinkled as he smiled. "It's a pleasure to finally meet the woman who has gotten this old dog to behave."

Bridget couldn't help but grin as she shook the manager's hand. "It's a pleasure to meet you, too. The event is lovely."

"And she's well-mannered." The man's white-as-snow brows lifted as he clapped Chad on the shoulder. "You're a lucky boy. I hope to see her at the games in the spring."

Chad replied, but Bridget really didn't hear him. Forcing her smile to remain on her face, she hated the suddenly heavy feeling in her chest. She wouldn't be at the games in the spring. Or if she happened to go to one—which she doubted she would—it wouldn't be in the context the manager hoped for.

Heart heavy, she excused herself to find the ladies' room. It was blissfully empty as she smoothed down some of the flyaways that were popping up all over her head and ordered herself to pull it together. She hadn't wanted to do this in the first place, and she should be thrilled it was almost over.

But she wasn't.

It had nothing to do with the glamorous life Chad lived—the dinners, the nights out, and all the attention. What she was going to miss was *him*.

Heading back into the ballroom, she got another glass of champagne, thinking the liquid courage could help, and scanned the glitzy room for Chad. There were so many men in tuxes it was like a sea of hotness. Shell was going to be so disappointed she didn't score an invite.

"Excuse me," came a soft, feminine voice.

Turning to the sound, she discovered she was surrounded by what you typically found in a sea of male hotness—its counterpart. The beach of ridiculously hot babes.

Bridget squared her shoulders, expecting an onslaught of catty remarks and probably a lecture on how bad Chad was at relationships. God only knew if he'd slept with any of these women.

"You must be Bridget." A slender blonde extended a delicate hand. Dressed in a tiny black dress, she looked like a movie star next to Bridget. "We've been hearing so much about you."

"Not from Chad. He's not the kiss-and-tell type," another woman said. Bridget thought her name was Tori from an earlier introduction.

"I love the dress," another woman said, her slanted eyes heavily lined with kohl. "It's such a beautiful color."

Bridget opened her mouth but was unsure of what to say.

"I'm so glad he's found someone," a raven-haired beauty said. "Chad needs a good woman."

Bridget was stunned.

A woman with toffee-colored skin stepped forward with a wide smile. "I'm sorry. You're probably like, what the hell with all of us converging on you. We just get excited whenever there's a chance we might outnumber the men. My name is Vanessa." She extended a hand. "My husband is number fifteen—shortstop. Drew Berry."

Bridget took the hand, recognizing the husband's name. "It's nice to meet you."

Vanessa smiled broadly and made a round of introductions

that were a blur to Bridget. "We should do brunch sometime or dinner—you work, right?"

She nodded as another woman grinned. "Or will Chad let you out of his sight long enough? Because he looks like the kind of man who likes to keep his woman busy."

A flush crept across her face an instant before Chad came up behind her, slipping an arm around her waist. "You doing okay over here?" he whispered, and when she nodded, he spoke louder, addressing the horde of beautiful and surprisingly nice women. "All of you look lovely tonight."

Vanessa's eyes rolled. "Chad—forever the charmer."

"He needs to talk to my husband," Tori added, and several of the women laughed. "You know what Bobby said to me tonight? That I looked like the best cut of steak." Her eyes rolled. "You can take the boy out of Texas, but you can't take Texas out of the boy."

"Being compared to steak is one of the highest forms of flattery," Chad explained, giving them his best grin. The one that hooked, lined, and sunk about a thousand women. "I hate to do this, but I'm going to steal Bridget."

"Have fun." Vanessa smiled. "I have to go find my husband. Our babysitter charges by the *half hour*. I'm pretty sure we've paid for her college by now."

After a round of good-byes and a promise to get Vanessa's phone number to set up brunch—people still ate brunch?—she was alone with Chad again.

He tucked back a wild curl. "You ready to get out of here?"

"Only if you are," she said. Even though her heels

were killing her, she didn't want to rush him off. And besides, when every evening ended, it brought them one more night—

She cut herself off.

"I am." He took the glass from her. "Let's see if we can make a clean escape."

She let him take her hand, and keeping to the edges of the ballroom, they made it all the way outside before anyone noticed them. A light snow had begun to fall as they hurried past the waiting photographers.

Chad buckled her in again, which caused a flurry of cameras to go off. She shot him a dirty look, which he returned with a smug, knowing grin.

Once inside the Jeep, he turned to her. "So how do you think tonight went?"

Assuming he meant his contract, she smiled as she slipped the shawl off and folded it in her lap. "I think you're not going to have any problems. Everyone seems impressed with the new, more behaved Chad."

He chuckled. "I wasn't talking about that. I meant in general."

"Oh." Her smile spread. "It was so much fun. People were really nice."

"Were you expecting them not to be?"

She considered that. "I guess so." Then she laughed. "Vanessa invited me out to brunch."

His answering grin warmed her. "You should go."

"Not . . ." She trailed off.

"Hmm?"

She shrugged. It seemed obvious to her, but maybe Chad

wasn't even thinking about it in the way she was. And she needed to stop thinking about it completely.

Glancing at him, she was struck again by his masculine beauty. Even while he was driving, the look of concentration that pulled down his brows and narrowed his eyes stirred heat within her.

She thought about what he'd done to her—for her—in the dressing room.

Her pulse picked up.

Maybe it was the memories of his wonderful fingers and the pleasure he had given her. Maybe it was the champagne she'd drunk and the great evening she had with him. Maybe it was because Chad was hot, and she wanted to do for him what he had done for her.

Who knew what gave her the idea, but Bridget was going to go with number three and not look back. She'd decided some time tonight that she wanted as many memories as she could gather before their time together ended. She'd need them for the cold winter nights alone in her near future.

So before she lost her nerve, she reached over while they waited at a red stoplight, placing her hand on his upper thigh. Chad's head whipped in her direction. One single brow went up. She gave him what she hoped was a sexy smile.

His eyes locked with hers, and Bridget took a deep breath. Blood pounding, she slid her hand up his leg and cupped him through his trousers.

Chad's hips buckled, and he groaned. "What . . . what are you doing, Bridget?"

She bit down on her lip as she ran her thumb up his

length. The man was already hard as a rock. "Just repaying you."

"Repaying me?" he said hoarsely.

Leaning over farther, she got her other hand involved in the fun and pulled the zipper down. The button was next and—holy momma—Chad was commando and all but straining toward her. Bridget's gaze drifted up. "The light's green, Chad."

"Yeah, green means go." He hit the gas, but he was barely doing the speed limit.

She eased him out of his pants, sliding her hand up and down his hard length. Moisture built at the tip, increasing each time she smoothed her thumb over its head. It wasn't long before his hips were moving up into her touch, his knuckles white from gripping the steering wheel.

And she wasn't done with him.

When they hit another red light, she unhooked her seat belt. Chad's eyes widened with realization. She gave him a little smile and then bent over, taking him into her mouth.

"Oh hell," Chad ground out.

His hips pumped up, and she loved that—loved the salty, masculine taste of him. Wrapping her hand around his base, she slid it up while her mouth went down, taking him as far as she could.

"Bridget, you . . ." Chad groaned. "This was probably the worst and . . ." He sucked in a breath. "The best idea you've had."

She moaned around him, and he made a low sound deep in his throat. His hand landed on her head, wrapping his fingers through her hair. It wasn't long before he was guiding her speed. When she flicked her tongue over his head again and his body jerked, she had no idea how he didn't wreck.

A shudder ran up his body. "Bridget, if you don't stop, I'm gonna . . ."

That's what she wanted. Tightening her hold, she pumped faster as she pulled her lips back, scraping his sensitive head with her teeth.

And that did it.

She felt his release rock through his body. He tried to lift her head, but Bridget wasn't having it. She was in this to the finish, and boy did she finish him. When she finally lifted her head, she saw that they were going about ten miles an hour and Chad looked like he just rolled out of bed.

His eyes slid to hers.

Bridget licked her lips.

"Fuck," he groaned out.

Smiling, she tucked his semi-hard sex back into his pants, zipped, and buttoned him up. "Do I need to drive?"

"No. No. I got this." He put both hands on the steering wheel and nodded. "Yeah, I got this."

Feeling warm and pleased with herself, Bridget redid her seat belt and settled back.

Several moments passed before Chad seemed able to speak again. "Wow. That was— There are no words." A lopsided grin appeared on his lips. "It's a damn good thing no photo-hags got a picture of that, though."

In that moment, Bridget forgot everything. Turning to

him, she laughed out loud. "Yeah, I doubt Miss Gore would be pleased with *those* pictures."

The day before Christmas Eve was a lazy day at work. Employees always cut out around three or earlier. Nothing got done, but that was okay, because Bridget and Madison were ready for the Gala and that was all that mattered.

So Bridget played Solitaire on her computer and tended her crops on Farmville until she found herself staring at her computer, thinking about Chad.

Goodness, he'd looked amazing at the event—the whole night had been amazing. A stupid, silly grin appeared on her face.

The Christmas dinner for the Nationals had been perfect and Chad . . . She wanted to pat herself on the back for what went down in his Jeep. She had been pretty damn perfect herself.

Though, it probably wasn't smart to do anything like that again. Even she'd said they shouldn't complicate things, but she figured she owed him. When he'd dropped her off at her apartment, she'd made a hasty exit, knowing that if she stayed a moment longer, the night would've ended in sex.

Her phone rang, startling her enough that she jerked back from the computer. "Office of Madison Daniels, how can I help you?"

"Miss Rodgers, can you see Director Bernstein please?"

Bridget felt like a tool, since she should've known it was an internal call. "Yes. I'll be right there."

Assuming he wanted something to do with the Gala, she shut down her web and went ahead and powered off the computer. The desks outside of Madison's office were empty. Robert was nowhere to be seen.

Swinging a left, she squeezed past a Christmas tree and entered Director Bernstein's office. His secretary glanced up with smile. "Go ahead in," she said.

Bridget pushed open the door and realized the director wasn't alone. Madison was with him, and she looked pissed. Her stomach sunk as she sat next to her boss. "What's going on?"

Director Bernstein smiled, but it looked pained, as if he were about to say something he really didn't want to. "I know you've worked very hard and closely with Miss Daniels on the Winter Fund-raiser Gala, and there really is no amount of gratitude that I can express. Both of you have done a superb job."

Bridget glanced over at Madison, having a feeling that whatever this conversation was truly about had nothing to do with his gratitude.

"The Gala is so important to the institute and for the volunteer process," the director continued. "Each year, we see an increase in attendees and donations and those donations are what keep departments like the one Miss Daniels oversees running. We cannot afford to lose any donors who wish to have a nice evening at the Gala without the intrusion of press."

Ice drenched Bridget's veins as she stared at her boss's boss. She forced herself to take a nice, slow breath. This had to do with Chad. Of course, everything had to do with Chad now, her *fake* boyfriend.

Whatever warm and fuzzy thoughts she had about him

minutes before vanished like the doughnuts Madison had brought in this morning.

"Keeping that in mind, I'm going to have to ask that you not attend the Gala, Miss Rodgers." That damn smile of his wavered. "Anything that involves Chad Gamble turns into a media circus, and many of our attendees do not want to be a part of an environment like that."

Madison cleared her throat and said, "Just so you know, I do not agree with this at all."

Funny how Bridget's cheeks were burning when she felt so cold inside, but she'd be damned if this crap with Chad ruined something she'd been working on all year. Although, he'd seemed to be looking forward to attending the Gala with her, she knew he wouldn't be too upset about being cut out of it. "He doesn't have to attend," she said. "I can do this without him."

Director Bernstein leaned forward, folding his hands on wood so polished Bridget could see her reflection in it. "I've considered that, but with or without Mr. Gamble, the press will follow you. How many days are they waiting outside to get just a photograph of you alone?"

Five, but who was counting? Bridget's hand curled uselessly in her lap. "I can try to talk to some of them. Ask them to stay away."

"You and I both know that's not going to work. They're like vultures, and if they think there's a chance they can film you and Mr. Gamble together, then they'll be camping outside. I cannot have that kind of negative press in attendance. I'm sorry, but it's in the best interest of the Gala and the Institute."

Bridget wasn't sure what she said next, but she was sure she'd nodded, agreed, and then the awkward-as-hell meeting was over. She was in a stupor as she went back to her office and grabbed her purse.

Madison looked as bad as Bridget felt. "I'm so sorry, Bridget. Bernstein is a huge Nationals fan—"

"It's okay." It really wasn't, and the last thing she wanted to hear was how the director fanboyed Chad in private. "Really. I tried talking him out of it, but there're a lot of conservative stiffs that come to this thing and donate a ton of money."

Forcing a smile she didn't feel, she gave her friend a brief hug. "It's okay. Hey, I'm going to get out of here. Have a good Christmas, okay?"

"Bridge—"

She walked out of the office, blinking back tears, but her head was high.

As she climbed into her car, she sent Chad a quick text, checking to see if he was home. The response was a quick yes and the drive to his posh apartment was a blur. She figured dis-inviting Chad from the Gala was best done in person.

He answered on the first knock and stepped aside, allowing her to come in the foyer. She quickly averted her gaze from him, because really, no man should look as good as he did in a plain shirt and lounge pants.

"I . . ." She took a deep breath and smelled Chinese food. Her brows pinched as she glanced around. "Why do I smell General Tso's chicken?"

Chad smiled. "When you said you were swinging by, I

took the liberty of ordering a late lunch. It's your favorite, right?"

Bridget winced at the considerate gesture. She wasn't hungry, which was testament to how sucky she was feeling right now. "Thank you, but I wasn't planning to stay very long."

He'd stopped halfway down the hall and turned to her, his brows furrowing. "That's— Hey, are you okay?"

She probably should've checked her face for smudged mascara. "Yes, I'm okay. I came here to tell you . . . to ask if you wouldn't attend the Gala." Not seeing the need to add the embarrassing part where she also wasn't attending, she stumbled along awkwardly. Maybe a phone call or text would've been better. "I know it's kind of rude to ask that of you and all, but I'd really appreciate it."

"Yeah. Okay." Chad leaned against the wall, folding his arms. "Did something happen with the Gala?"

She shook her head, still way too emotional to go into details, and seriously, it wasn't like he really cared. Dating was a job to him right now, and she doubted he'd appreciate her going all drama llama on him. No one had agreed to that in the beginning.

"Did someone say something to you?"

Heat crawled up her neck. Goodness, he could be astute at times. "No. It . . . just is. Anyway, that's all I came by for, but I really need to get going. Um, thanks for the Chinese. Rain check on that?"

"Wait." He pushed off the wall, coming at her. "What time do you want me to pick you up tomorrow?"

"Tomorrow?" she repeated, searching her memory for plans. "Tomorrow is Christmas Eve . . . ?"

A quirky grin appeared. "Yeah, and I always spend it with Maddie's family, along with my brothers."

Oh, Madison's family Christmas celebration. She'd managed to avoid that like the plague the last couple of years.

"You're going with me, right?" he said after a few moments, clearly choosing to ignore the fact she'd already shot his offer down once before.

Bridget pursed her lips. "Christmas Eve dinners are not my thing."

"Well, it's not really traditional. Actually it's the opposite of traditional. Mostly it's just drinking and snacking and watching Chase get drunk and make a fool out of himself."

"As fun as that sounds, I'm going to have to pass." She started backing toward the door. "But I hope you have a good time."

"Hold on." He put his hand on the door, stopping her. "What's your deal? I'm cool with the Gala thing and I'll take the rain check on the Chinese, so would it kill you to go to this with me?"

"Yes," she snapped, reaching for the door handle. "Chad, come on. Open the door."

"You know, sometimes I think I get you and then I realize I don't have a freaking clue. You like Maddie and Chase, so it shouldn't be a big deal." He removed his hand from the door and thrust it through his hair. "It's like you don't want to . . . I don't know, open yourself up."

"Open myself up?"

Chad frowned. "Yeah."

Bridget didn't know what made the words come out of

her mouth. The holidays always had her on edge and mix in all of this with Chad and the Gala, her patience and filter were nonexistent. "Why do you want me to go with you, Chad? Why would you want me to open myself up to you? It's not like we're really dating, and the last thing we should be doing is spending the holidays together or getting deep and meaningful with each other when it's going to be all over soon anyway."

"Whoa. Wow." Chad reached around her, opening the door so she could dip under his arm. "That's fine. Wouldn't want to get all deep and meaningful, Bridget. You're right. This'll be over in days. Why bother?"

She blanched. "Exactly."

"Whatever. Have a nice Christmas, Bridget." And then he closed the door. He didn't even slam it, which seemed worse somehow.

Chapter Eighteen

The Daniels' house looked like Christmas got drunk and threw up on it.

There was a blowup Santa, one of those weird ones that reminded Chad of Bubble Boy, in the front yard. Wire reindeer glimmered in the night, flashing white and then red. On the roof was another Santa, perched near the chimney. There was a blowup sleigh on the other patch of frozen grass. Christmas lights in every color imaginable hung from the roof and circled the porch railing. A backlit Frosty the Snowman was waving at him. Creepy. On the porch was Frank E. Post, which kicked on and started singing "Have a Swinging Christmas" when Chad came within a few feet of it.

"Whoa," he said, stepping around that thing.

Before he knocked on the door, he shook out his shoulders, trying to lose the pissy attitude he'd been rocking since yesterday courtesy of Bridget. How foolish did he look getting all . . . considerate and shit by ordering her favorite food and then assuming she'd want to spend Christmas Eve with him?

He should've known better. They were faking this whole

dating thing. He just hadn't thought about that when she'd texted him. Little did he know she was coming over to ask him *not* to go to the Gala with her.

Whatever. He wasn't going to let this crap with Bridget ruin the one night a year he was actually surrounded by family.

His brother answered the door, decked out in a sweater that had Chad laughing so hard he was afraid he was going to drop the gifts he'd brought. Bright green with a knitted jolly Saint Nick, holding a sign that read: EVEN SANTA IS PREPARED 4 ARMAGEDDON. R U? MERRY CHRISTMAS!

"If you say one word," Chase said, holding open the door, "I will kick your ass."

Maddie's father popped out and gave a huge wave. He wore the same sweater. "Hey there, all-star!"

Chad struggled to get the smile off his face. "I won't say a word."

"I bet." Chase took one of the bags from him and then frowned. "Where's Bridget?"

He followed his younger brother in. The air smelled of Old Bay seasoning and beer—a Daniels' Christmas Eve tradition. "She couldn't make it."

"Hmm," Chase replied, putting the bags down by the tree.

Chad turned, hoping to make a hasty escape before his brother could start asking more questions. He was enveloped in a warm hug.

"I'm so glad you could make it," Mrs. Daniels said, squeezing the damn life out of him, but man, he loved those hugs. She pulled back, the skin crinkling around her eyes as she smiled. "Is it possible that you get more handsome every time I see you?"

"Ew, Mom!" Maddie's voice carried from the kitchen.

"It's entirely possible, Mrs. Daniels." Chad winked.

Mr. Daniels swung an arm over his wife's shoulder. The man was as huge as a bear. His apocalypse-ready Santa was at least three times bigger than Chase's. "Sorry, Chad, I try to keep her paws off you."

"Oh, he knows my eyes and hands are for you." To prove her words, she grabbed Mr. Daniels' ass.

Mitch poked his head out and curled his lips in horror. "Not something I wanted to see. Ever."

Mr. Daniels huffed. "Yeah, well, you've obviously been grabbing a lot more than your wife's—"

"Dad," Mitch groaned. "Really?"

From beside the Christmas tree, Mitch's wife Lissa grinned and rubbed her swollen belly. "It's true."

"My family's insane." Mitch disappeared back into the hall.

They were, but Chad loved them—loved the whole warm atmosphere. It was one of the reasons why he and his brothers had been drawn to their family. It was the complete opposite of theirs.

Speaking of family, Chandler came out and shoved a cold one in his hand. He noted that he wasn't rocking a Daniels's Christmas sweater. "Where's your woman?"

Chad sighed, not wanting to think about Bridget. "She's not here."

His brother nodded curtly. With his hair pulled back in a small ponytail at the nape of his neck, Chandler looked like the kind of guy people hired security to protect them *from*. "What about the other one?"

"Other one?"

"Yeah—the one with glasses?" he clarified.

Chad's brows shot up. "Miss Gore—my publicist? Who knows? I'm just hoping it's far away from me. Wait. You're not—"

Before he could finish that nightmare of a sentence, Maddie appeared with a platter of cookies, eyes narrowed. "Oh, what the hell? Where is Bridget?"

"She couldn't make it," Chase tossed over his shoulder, sending Chad a look as he took the tray from Maddie. "Or that's what Chad claims."

Maddie looked like she was about to throw something. "Every year I invite her, and this was the one year I figured she had no way of escaping."

"Sorry." Chad shrugged. "I guess she's scared you guys will lock her in a bomb shelter or something."

She rolled her eyes. "That's not why she won't come."

Curiosity was definitely piqued. "You mean she's not afraid you guys are going to force feed her freeze-dried survival food?"

"Ha. Ha. No."

"Then why does she bail?" he asked.

Maddie glanced over her shoulder. At that moment, Mr. Daniels had Chase and Chandler cornered, showing them some survival magazine. Maddie winced and grabbed his arm, pulling him into the empty kitchen. On the stove, a huge pot of shrimp steamed.

"Bridget doesn't like Christmas."

Chad crossed his arms. "I figured as much."

"Do you know why? Probably not, because she doesn't talk about it."

"Are you going to tell me?" He leaned against the counter.

She sighed. "I'm only telling you this because I love that girl to death, and she had a really crappy day yesterday."

"Wait. What do you mean?"

Maddie looked dumbfounded. "She didn't tell you? Of course not." She shook her head as Chad's patience stretched. "You know how we've been working on the Gala and it's been our life for almost the last year."

Chad knew Bridget's job hung on the line.

"We're still a lot of money short, which has the director insane about the Gala. He pulled her into a meeting yesterday," she said. "She's not allowed to attend the fund-raiser."

"What?" He straightened his arms. "Why the fuck not?"

Maddie looked uncomfortable. "It's because of you."

"Excuse me?"

She cringed. "See, the director is concerned about you two kind of taking over the event, it becoming more about you being there than raising money, and there's going to be a lot of conservative people there who won't want their pictures taken—"

"Bridget came by yesterday and asked that I not go, but she didn't say anything about this." Anger had his hands clenching. "I'm not going. It should be an easy fix."

"Yeah, that's what Bridge said, but he knows the press still could be there. He's not going to let her go."

Why hadn't Bridget told him this? "That's absolute bullshit. She deserves to go."

"I know. I totally agree, but what the director says goes. There's nothing I can do." Maddie turned her head to the side a bit. "I should've figured she wouldn't tell you. Probably didn't want you to feel bad."

Fuck. He felt like an ass. Bridget hadn't given him a reason for asking him not to attend, but if he'd known it had been because of him . . .

"Anyway," Maddie said. "This time of year isn't good for her. So the whole Gala thing is definitely adding to it."

Chad thrust his fingers through his hair. "Why doesn't she like Christmas?"

There was a pause. "Her parents were killed on Christmas Eve when she was in college."

"Holy shit . . ."

"I didn't know how it was before then, but ever since I've known her, she doesn't celebrate Christmas. Bad memories, I guess, but I've been trying to give her new ones, you know?" She looked crestfallen. "I was hoping since she was dating you, the holidays could actually be something nice for her."

Chad stared at Maddie. Bridget had told him her parents had passed during one of their dates, but he hadn't known how or the timing. Good God, no wonder Christmas sucked for her and on top of that, her director pulling her out of the Gala?

He was pissed and he was also . . . he was also upset.

Turning to the pot on the stove, he tried to imagine what it was like for Bridget right now and he could easily. Before he had the Daniels family, Christmas wasn't celebrated. There were no goofy sweaters, gifts, laughter ringing through the house, or shrimp boiling on the stove. Christmas at the Gambles had been cold and as sterile as everything else. Except his mother was usually more doped up and his father would almost always be away on a "business trip," but this was different.

Different on so many levels.

None of this should really affect him, but it did. He was upset *for* Bridget, and he didn't want her sitting at home alone. He also didn't want her not to be able to see a year's worth of work not come to fruition

Chad wanted to fix this. Strange—really fucking strange, because typically whatever problems he faced, he either ignored them or blew right through them. Or someone else took care of them. He never really fixed them.

But he was going to fix the fuck out of this.

One thing he could do now. The other, which involved a phone call to his accountant and then to the rat bastard of a director, would have to wait.

"Chad?" came Maddie's quiet voice.

He turned around, his mind made up. "I have to go. Can you pass my regrets to your family?"

Maddie blinked slowly, and then her eyes were aglow with happiness. "Yeah—yes, I can."

He started past her, but she called out his name, stopping him. "What are you going to do?"

Chad wasn't 100 percent sure, but he only knew one thing. "I'm going to go make new memories."

* * *

It was damn near eight o'clock in the evening before Bridget decided she needed to shower and brush her teeth, but the marathon of *The Walking Dead* had kept her glued to the screen for most of the day.

And nothing, not even hygiene, was more important than the cray cray of a zombie infestation.

Seemed funny to be finally taking off her jammies to shower and put fresh pajamas back on, but that's what she was doing.

Tying the sash on her robe loosely around her waist, she patted out most of the water in her hair with her towel as she crossed her living room and peered out on the streets down below. There was last-minute traffic congesting the streets, but in about an hour, there'd be nothing, and tomorrow, there'd only be a few cars carrying people to see their families.

Bridget had decided to go to the movies tomorrow and eat as much popcorn as she could stomach.

Moving away from the window, she dropped the towel on the back of the recliner and glanced at the coffee table. Her cell phone had been so silent that Pepsi had curled up around it.

She briefly toyed with the idea of texting Chad a Merry Christmas message as she planned on doing, but after the complete hideous bitch she'd been to him yesterday, she doubted he'd be happy to hear from her.

Chad had actually tried to be considerate and sweet with the food thing, and she had . . . well, she just had a really bad day.

Bridget sincerely hoped he was having a good time and

tried not to think past the New Year, but it was inevitable. How many dates did they have left in them? Three. Maybe four, and then nothing.

And considering how she sounded yesterday, Chad probably thought she didn't even care.

Sitting down on the couch, she picked up the remote and searched for something on the TV to distract her. When that failed, she tried searching out a favorite book of hers from the case.

A sudden, unexpected knock on the door caused her to drop the book. Pepsi popped up from the coffee table, kicking her cell phone onto the floor as he darted into the bedroom.

Bridget sighed.

Having no idea who could be here other than a neighbor, she peered through the little peephole in her door.

Air punched out of her lungs, and her heart skipped a beat.

She'd recognized that back of a head anywhere.

Chapter Nineteen

Opening the door, she stared, dumbfounded and confused. What was he doing here? She couldn't even fathom.

Chad turned around, holding a box in his arms. His eyes deepened to a midnight blue the moment they met hers. Without saying a word, he eased past her. She shut the door and turned around, leaning against the door.

It took her a couple of moments to remember how to speak. "What are you doing here?"

Chad glanced around her tiny apartment with interest. "It's Christmas Eve."

"Yeah, I know that." God, she would've straightened up a little if she had known he was going to swing by. "Shouldn't you be with your brothers and Madison's family?"

He shrugged as he placed a box on the coffee table. Something festive-sounding jingled inside. Sitting down on her couch like he'd done it a million times before, he grinned up at her as he patted the cushion next to him. He grinned. "I like the paint by the way. Miss Gore said it looked like *Sesame Street* in here, but I don't think so."

Oh, Lord help her, she hated that woman. Her gaze

bounced from the blue to the red walls. Okay. It kind of did remind her of *Sesame Street*. "You don't?"

"Nope. I like it. It fits you."

Her little heart got all a-fluttery at the sound of that, which was bad and so needed to stop. "What are you doing here, Chad?"

"Sit." He patted the spot beside him again.

"You're not leaving, are you?" She winced as she caught sight of Pepsi peeking out from the bedroom.

"Nope."

More nervous than she'd ever been in her entire life, she tugged the robe a little closer and sat down beside him. He leaned back and tipped his head toward her. His gaze traveled over her damp hair and then moved to the vee in the robe before going to the belt she was grasping like a lifeline. "I should've swung by about ten minutes earlier."

Bridget wanted to laugh, but then she remembered—not that she'd really forgotten—what they had done in the Jeep after dinner. Er, what she had done, actually. Each time they did something, she told herself it wouldn't happen again. It was a useless mantra as she watched him out of the corner of her eyes.

Without warning, a blob of orange jumped up onto the arm of the couch. Chad turned, brows rising as Pepsi stared back at him. "That is the biggest cat I've ever seen."

As if Pepsi had understood the difference between *big* and *fat*, the cat eased down off the arm and tentatively approached Chad. She held her breath.

Chad reached out and scratched the cat behind his ear. "What's his name?"

"Pepsi."

"Pepsi?" Chad laughed. "Why that name?"

She smiled. "I found him in a Pepsi case when he was a kitten. The name stuck." Surprise flickered through her as Pepsi climbed onto Chad's lap. "I'm shocked that he's letting you pet him. He's not that friendly."

Chad glanced at her, a wicked gleam. "What can I say? Pussies love me."

A short laugh burst from her. "I cannot believe you just said that."

"Yeah, that was kind of bad." He ran his hand over Pepsi's belly. A few moments passed in silence, and then he said casually, "Madison told me."

"Told you what?" Her stomach immediately knotted.

He threw an arm along the back of the couch, his fingers catching a strand of damp hair. "About your parents."

Looking away, she took a deep breath. "So you're here because you feel sorry for me? Because if that's the case, you can save your sympathy. I don't want pity. It's why I don't talk about—"

"Hey there . . ." He gently tugged on the strand of hair. "I do feel sorry for you, but it's not pity. It's empathy."

She turned to him, brows raised. "Empathy?"

He smiled his lopsided grin as he continued to shower Pepsi with attention. "Yeah, you're surprised that I know what that means, right? But I do. And there's nothing wrong with feeling empathy for you."

Bridget stared at him.

"And what happened to your parents sucks. And the fact that you can't enjoy something like Christmas is even worse." Chad twirled the hair around his finger, and she found that she liked it when he played with her hair. "I get why you don't want to. At first, I was against the whole Daniels clan Christmas party, even when I was a kid. You know, it was Chase who started hanging out with Mitch first. Chandler and I were older and thought we were too cool, but the Daniels invited us over one Christmas Eve and we were like, what the hell?"

Bridget settled back against the couch, quiet as he talked. What was rarer than her talking about her parents was Chad talking about his and his childhood. In a way, they kind of had that in common. Their families and pasts were something both of them held close, and they respected that about each other.

"It was strange being around a family—a normal, happy family." His gaze left hers, centering on the box on the table. "My parents really didn't celebrate anything. Both of them were too wrapped up in their own worlds really to care for much else. When my brothers and I were really little, they'd put some stuff up for Christmas, but that stopped as soon as my father . . ."

He didn't need to elaborate. Bridget already knew from what Madison had told her. The senior Gamble had been a well-known businessman, controlling and hard-partying, and if someone looked up the definition of *womanizing* in the dictionary, their father's picture would've been under it.

"Anyway, once I started going to the Daniels house for the holidays, I was glad I did. And I know you have your reasons. I respect that, but you shouldn't be alone on Christmas."

"Chad . . ." She didn't know what to say as she watched him gently place Pepsi on the cushion next to him and sit forward. Her heart was pounding in her chest like she'd just run circles around her living room.

"And I've spent a dozen or so Christmas Eves with the Danielses and more than I want to remember with my brothers." He flashed that teasing smile of his. "And I haven't spent one with you. So that's why I'm here. Don't argue with me about it."

Her fingers loosened around the robe as she shook her head. Part of her was dancing around like a hippie chick, but the other part was terrified—scared senseless by this act of kindness and caring.

And then he opened up the box.

"This is what my mom used to put up in the house for Christmas. It's kind of dumb and really pathetic, but I always liked the stupid thing." Chad pulled out a faint green ceramic Christmas tree about two feet tall. Each limb had a tiny bulb attached to it. An electrical plug dangled from the base. "Pretty cornball, huh? But this was our tree for years."

Tears filled her eyes as he got up and sat the tree on the end table and then plugged it in. The little tree lit from within, glowing a soft green, and the multicolored bulbs glimmered.

"Ta-da!" He straightened and faced Bridget. The wide smile immediately faded. "Oh no . . ."

"I'm sorry." She dabbed at the corners of her eyes with the sleeves of her robe. "I don't mean to cry. I'm not upset."

He looked more confused by each passing second.

"This is just such a nice thing," she hastily added. "I love the tree, really, I do. Thank you."

And she was pretty sure in that moment she knew there was no turning back. She had fallen hard for him, irrevocably so. Nothing was going to change that. Not even the fact that their whole relationship was built on lies.

Bridget was in love with him.

That realization couldn't have come at a better or worse time. Her heart was swelling while her brain was plotting ways to kick the ever-loving crap out of her. Falling for Chad was so dangerous to her heart, but she couldn't help it.

Her heart didn't belong to her anymore.

It belonged to the man in front of her.

Chad's grin was a little unsure, something she'd never seen before. "Man, if you're going to cry over that, I better find some tissues."

Bridget started laughing. "Why?"

"Prepare yourself." Chad reached back in the box and pulled out a small red box wrapped with red satin. "I got you something."

"Oh, Chad, you shouldn't have."

He arched a brow. "You haven't even seen what it is."

"But I didn't—"

"I don't care that you didn't get me something. That's not what this is about." He sat back down, and Pepsi rolled over against his leg like a blob of orange fat and fur. "And besides, you've pretty much given me my future with the team, even if you agreed to do this to increase your dating pool."

Bridget opened her mouth, because that so wasn't the reason why, but she couldn't tell if he was teasing or not, and how could she admit to the truth?

She was basically blackmailed. What a mood killer.

Chad placed the little box in her hand. Very carefully, she hooked her pinkie under the ribbon and pulled. It slid off easily, and then she pried off the lid.

Bridget sucked in a sharp breath. "Oh my God . . ."

"I'll take that as you like it?"

"Like it . . . ?" Bridget reached inside and with shaking fingers, she lifted the necklace she would've skipped rent to get. It was the one from the Little Boutique; the emerald on the silver chain.

Chad took the box from her and placed it on the coffee table. "That is the one you were looking at in the store, right?"

"Yes," she breathed, blinking back fresh tears. "Why would you do this?"

"Because I wanted to."

"And you always do what you want?" The jewel was the perfect weight.

"Not always," he said quietly. "I used to think I did and maybe I did, but not anymore—not always."

She lifted damp lashes and her eyes locked with his. "Thank you. You shouldn't have, but thank you. And I'm sorry about yesterday. I was such a bitch and you were just being nice. I'm sorry—

"Hey, it's no big deal." Chad reached forward and took the necklace from her hands. "Turn around and lift your hair."

Twisting at the waist, she obeyed and lifted the heavy mass of hair. Chad was quiet and quick as he moved. It was only the cool slide of the emerald between her breasts that alerted her to his closeness. Then the necklace must've been clasped, because his hands were around hers, lowering them so that her hair came down over her shoulders. He let go, though.

Bridget faced him, her heart and pulse pounding in every part of her body. She didn't know what she was doing.

Leaning forward, she placed her hands on the small section of the couch between them, and she pressed her lips to his. "Thank you," she said again, and pulled back. There was no mistaking the hunger in those cobalt eyes.

Chad said nothing as she stood on suddenly shaky legs. In the dark room lit only by the muted TV and the little Christmas tree, Bridget knew she didn't want him to leave. Not yet. Not ever. And she also knew she'd only get one of those things.

Her fingers found the emerald, and her chest spasmed. "Would you like something to drink? I think I have some wine or—"

He was on his feet so suddenly that Pepsi shot off the couch and into the kitchen, and Bridget felt a thrill of excitement. There was no mistaking the intent in his expression.

"I am thirsty," he said, taking a step forward.

Bridget was breathless as she moved back. She didn't make it very far. He was in front of her in seconds, cupping her cheeks. He kissed her, as quickly and gently as she had kissed him . . . and she was undone.

"Please . . . " she whispered.

He grew very still. "Please what?"

She wetted her lips, and Chad's groan rumbled through both of them. "Touch me, but don't stop. Please."

Chapter Twenty

His hands slipped down her neck and landed on her shoulders. Tipping his chin down, his fevered eyes met hers. "Are you sure that's what you want, Bridget? Because once I start, I won't stop again. I will take you—take you so hard that every breath afterward is only going to remind you of me."

Upon hearing those words, her heart tripped up and her body blossomed for him. Bridget nodded, because she was so beyond speaking. Nothing she'd say right now would make any sort of sense and would only serve to make her sound like a fool.

"Good—that's good," he said, sliding his hands down her front, stopping on the belt. "You have no idea how badly I've wanted this. Days. Weeks. Months now. I've wanted you—only you."

"Yes," she whispered huskily, discovering she was capable of saying that. "Yes."

He kissed her, tasted her lips and the recesses of her mouth as he tugged the sash loose. The robe parted and air rushed across skin that was bared as he brushed the heavy cloth off her shoulders, letting it fall to the floor.

Pulling back just enough to see her in nothing but the necklace he'd given her, he ran his hand between her breasts and belly in a tender gesture. "Have I told you how beautiful you are?"

Bridget nodded, mouth dry.

"I'm going to tell you again. You're beautiful. And you're perfect." He claimed her lips again as he gripped her hips. His arousal was fierce and hard.

They were moving backward as his hands found her rear and squeezed, and then his hands were everywhere, working her body like a fine-tuned instrument. She was putty in his hands, wet and ready.

Satisfaction and need slammed into Bridget as her back hit the wall, and he was pressed against her, his hips grinding. She reached down, hooking her fingers under his sweater. He lifted his hands long enough for her to tug the clothing off his head and then her skin was flush against his. She went for the top button on his jeans, her fingers brushing his arousal.

He growled against her parted lips as she eased the zipper down and freed him. She wrapped her hand around the hard, hot length, and his hips punched forward.

"Don't stop," she begged. "Please."

"Not planning to." Chad stepped out of his jeans and shoes. "But I love hearing you say please. Say it again."

Bridget ran her fingers down his taut, rippled abs. "Please."

He kissed her, sucking her lower lip into his mouth, and she pulsed between her legs. "Say it again," he ordered.

As his hand skated over her hip and landed solidly on her

rear, she moaned. Her whole body tingled—her nipples, skin, and her sex. "Please."

Suddenly, his arms were around her, and he was lifting her up. Her body knew what to do, wrapping its legs around his waist. There wasn't even a moment where she worried about how hard it must've been for him to pick her up. Instead, she felt light and feminine.

Chase spun around as he flicked his tongue against hers. "Bedroom?"

"Second door to the left."

"Gotcha."

They made it to her bedroom within record time. He stalked to the foot of her bed and held her there another moment as his kiss turned into something uninhibited, lush, and wet.

Chad went down on his knees on the mattress, and then she was on her back, staring up at him. He moved over her, his stare and controlled movements predatory. His arousal stood out, proud and commanding.

He kissed her once more before leaving her swollen lips and traveling south. She felt the soft tickle of his mouth against her throat and then on her collarbone. His breath huffed out against her breast, and his mouth then closed over her peak. Her back bowed off the mattress as he drew her in deep. She jerked her hips into his, feeling him sliding over her belly.

Bridget reached down, cupping him, and his breath faltered as he rubbed himself against her hand. "Chad, I need you."

A hand tightened on her hip. "That's all I want to hear—ever."

She didn't have a chance to digest what that meant. Sharp darts of pleasure shot through her as he slipped two fingers inside her. "You're so wet," he murmured, his eyes bright with heat. "I want to taste you, but fuck, I can't wait."

She nodded, deep anticipation stirring in her belly as he rose up, positioning an elbow beside her head. She felt him then, nudging at her core. She spread her thighs wider before thinking better of it. "Condom?"

"Are you on the pill?" he asked. "I've never been with anyone without a condom before, but I need to feel you. All of you, Bridget."

"Yes," she breathed.

His hot gaze traveled down her, resting at the spot where they were almost joined. "Beautiful," he murmured.

She raised her hips, desperate to bring them together, but he clamped a hand down on her hip and forced her back down.

"No."

"No?" she breathed.

A half-smile appeared on his lips as he dragged his gaze back up to hers. "Not yet."

Was he expecting her to wait? Because she didn't want to wait—not for this and not for him. She reached forward, about to force them to join. With reflexes honed from years on the field, he rose to his knees and caught her hands just as her fingers brushed his waist. He brought her wrists together in one grip, forcing her arms above her head.

Her heart tripled in speed. "What are you doing?"

"Getting ready to fuck you."

"That's not what it looks like to me."

He chuckled in a way that made her think of dark and sinful things and shifted so that his knees were between her spread thighs, forcing her open wide. "You just haven't been properly fucked yet."

Oh Lord . . .

Chad's gaze swept over her again, and she'd never felt more exposed, her body arched, her breasts thrusting up. She couldn't move her limbs, not with her arms held by him and her legs forced open. Instead of feeling self-conscious, she felt a delicious wave of awareness.

Mouth dry, she swallowed. "And are you going to fuck me properly?"

"Until you're senseless," he said, and then his head dipped. Those wonderful lips wrapped around her nipple as he reached between them, his clever fingers sliding down her belly, stopping just above where she wanted him.

Bridget whimpered.

He nipped at the peak of her breast, causing her to gasp. "What do you want, Bridget?"

"You know." Surely he didn't expect her to *talk* about this.

His teeth grazed her other nipple. Her body jerked. Then he soothed the sting with his warm tongue. He went back and forth, alternating between small bites of pain and soothing licks, until she squirmed from the relentless torture.

"Chad," she gasped, her eyes wide.

"Tell me what you want." His mouth went around her breast again, and he suckled deeply, drawing a hoarse cry from her. "Tell me, Bridget."

Her fingers curled helplessly. "I want you."

"No. Tell me what you want me to *do*."

She could barely breathe. "I want you . . . I want you to touch me."

"Yes." His tongue flicked over her sensitive nipple. "Tell me where you want me to touch you."

Jesus. There was a good chance she was going to smack him over the head after this. She considered refusing to answer him, but she was too needy and wanted him too badly. "I want you to touch me between my legs."

Chad hummed his approval and then his fingers were sliding over her aching sex, touching her but not enough. Nowhere near enough.

"More," she said—begged, really.

He sat back, brought her arms down so her wrists were pinned under her breasts with his one had. His gaze flicked up to her as he slowly, softly stroked her with one finger. "More?"

"Yes." Her chest was heaving now.

He slipped a finger inside her. "Is that what you wanted?" Before she could answer, he hooked his finger inside her and nearly set her off. "Do you still want more?"

Bridget would always want more. "Yes—please—yes."

A smug smile graced his lips as he eased another finger inside her, working her slowly at first and then harder and deeper.

"I like this." He watched her the entire time—his gaze locked on what he was doing. "I like watching you ride my hand. Fucking beautiful."

He did that hooking thing with his fingers again and between that and the way he watched her, he drove her insane and right to the brink of a huge release.

Chad pulled his hand away from her just as she started to quiver, and she cried out. When their gazes collided, he raised his fingers to his mouth, sucking off her arousal.

Bridget almost lost it then.

He made a low sound in his throat. "You taste so good I just have to have more."

Then his head was between her thighs, and that wonderful, wicked tongue of his delved deep between her folds. He speared her flesh, suckled from her like she was some kind of sweet nectar.

Her head was spinning, her hips grinding down on his mouth. She came close to release again, her breath ragged as her soft cries filled the room.

Chad stopped short just as she was about to break apart, lips glossy as he withdrew his fingers slowly. He moved his hand farther down, until one finger teased the sensitive, puckered skin. Her body tensed as a slew of erotic images assaulted her—of him taking her like that. Something she'd never done before.

"Later," he promised in a dark voice. "I'm going to own that too, but later."

Then he was moving up her, pinning her hands above her head again. He powered his hips forward, plunging deep inside her with one stroke. Bridget cried out, her fingers digging into her palms as he entered her. The minor bit of discomfort as her body adjusted to his size was nothing compared to the pleasure she knew was waiting. She lifted her hips, urging him on.

"Jesus, you're so tight," he growled as he pushed down.

Pleasure coiled tightly as he withdrew slowly and then

eased his way back in. She'd never felt so full before. He was slow at first, but the pace picked up and his hips were pounding into hers as she hooked her ankles behind his back.

"Chad!" she cried out as the orgasm tore through her, deep and fast, robbing her of breath.

He let go of her wrists then, grasping her hips and lifting her as he hammered into her. She gripped his shoulders as she shattered again, flew apart under his relentless strokes. Her sex pulsed and squeezed around his and then he came, his hard muscles flexing and tensing under her hands.

His heart was pounding against hers, just as fast. The brush of his lips was tender and so at odds with the fierceness that had rolled through both of them moments before.

He withdrew slowly and eased onto his side. She was a useless pile of bones and skin as he pulled her over to him, tucking her close so her head rested against his chest.

In the silence that followed, Bridget listened to his heart. She didn't know what to expect. For him to leave or go to sleep? She was never good at these kinds of things.

She lifted her head. "I'm . . . I'm going to get something to drink. Do you want anything?"

He pried one eye open. "I'll get it," he said, starting to sit up.

"No." She placed a hand on his chest. "I'll do it. I'll . . . uh, be right back."

Chad said nothing as she carefully untangled herself from him and grabbed a longish shirt from the pile of clean clothes folded on her chair. Slipping it on and padding out to the kitchen, she was somewhat pleased by the dull twinge between her legs.

The sex . . . well, it had been the best sex of her life.

She went to grab the wine and took her time searching for glasses. If Chad was planning on leaving, she was giving him enough time to get up. She wanted to avoid that awkward moment for her heart and pride.

Rising up on the tips of her toes, she reached for two wineglasses. The sudden heat behind her caused her heart to jump.

"Here," Chad said, reaching over her. "Let me help."

Bridget gripped the edges of the counter as he picked up the two glasses. He placed them beside the bottle, but instead of pouring the wine, he gripped her hips and pressed forward. She let out a gasp when she felt the length of him against her rear.

"Did you think one time was going to be enough?" A hand traveled up her back, wrapping around her hair. He guided her head back. Their eyes met and the room tilted. "Or did you think I was going to leave?"

She was past the pretense of lying. "Yes."

"Is that what you want?" He moved in, and his cock dipped, coming so close to where she was aching for him.

"No," she admitted. "But I thought—"

"You think too much." He kissed her, flicking his tongue over hers. "And you know what I think?"

Oh God . . . "What?"

"I hate this goddamn shirt." With that, he let go of her hair and the shirt was lying somewhere on the kitchen floor within seconds. "Ah, that's much better."

She pushed her hips back, her breath coming out in short puffs. "Is it?"

"Oh, yeah." He pulled her back more and then ran a hand down her spine, sending shivers dancing over her skin. "We're going to do this. Right here. It's going to be hard and rough. You ready?"

A bolt of pure lust exploded in her, priming her sex. Bridget nodded, her heart giving out a little as she tightened her grip on the counter. She stared at the cabinet door in front of her, eyes drifting half shut.

Chad splayed a hand across her belly and tugged her up. He made a guttural sound an instant before he slammed into her. She cried again, her back arching as she nearly came from the sweet, deep penetration. He slid out a few inches and repeated the movement until the only sounds in the apartment were their breathing and slamming of their bodies pushing against each other.

His fingers dug into her hips as he thrust forward, over and over. Their rhythm wasn't perfect, especially not when he reached up from around her and grabbed her breasts. His nimble fingers found her nipple and his teeth latched onto her shoulder.

Bridget screamed his name as her orgasm exploded through her body, like he had promised all those nights ago in the club, and he came with a deep groan, rocking and shuddering.

When he finally did pull out, which felt like an eternity later and still not long enough, he turned her around. "Are you okay?" Concern radiated from his tone.

"I'm perfect—that was perfect." She smiled, amazed she could still stand, though.

Chad looped his arms around her waist, and she saw

something shift in his expression before he lowered his head, kissing her slowly. The kissing inevitably led to other things. A touch against her breast, between her thighs, and they kept kissing as he turned her around and lifted her onto the kitchen table. Pushing forward, he split her thighs and his kisses traveled all the way down. Bridget's head fell back and her eyes closed as he did another thing he'd promised.

Chad worshipped her.

Sometime later, they ended up back in the bedroom, the wine forgotten and their limbs coated in sweat and tangled together.

"Merry Christmas," he said, pressing his lips to her damp forehead.

Bridget's chest spasmed as she snuggled closer. His arm around her waist tightened, and she squeezed her eyes shut against the sudden rush of tears.

This was going to end badly, because she knew that when it came time to let him go, it was going to be the last thing she ever wanted to do. Every part of her was relaxed and deliciously sated, but her heart . . . oh, it was aching something fierce.

She took a deep breath and pushed the lump in her throat down. "Merry Christmas, Chad."

Yeah, things were definitely complicated now.

Chad couldn't remember having a better Christmas morning. He woke up with his arm around Bridget's waist and his head buried in her hair. When he rolled her over, she smiled up at him sleepily and spread her thighs for him.

Fucking perfect.

He'd taken his time with her this morning, moving in her slowly, dragging the pleasure out for both of them. He wasn't fucking or screwing her. He knew what he was doing.

The shower had been a different story.

Chad had bent her over and drove into her like he'd never had sex before. Being with her, being inside of her, was something he would never get tired of. He knew that in his soul.

Lots of laughter and sex and some clothing later, they made breakfast together while Pepsi sat by the stove, waiting for scraps to fall to the floor.

He didn't know what it was about this whole setup, but he didn't want to be anywhere than where he was. It was when she was cuddled against him on the couch that he did he remember what else Maddie had told him last night.

Brushing the riot of waves back from her face, he grinned when her lashes lifted and yearning shone through her eyes. His own sex came roaring to life in a nanosecond. "Very soon," he promised both of them. "But first, there was something else that Maddie told me last night."

Bridget sat up, tucking her hair back. Her brows knitted. "What?"

"She told me about your director and how he doesn't want you to attend because of me. Look, I'm going to take—"

"Wait." She held up a hand. "I'll admit, I was pissed when the director pulled me out. I worked on that Gala all year, but there's something I need to tell you before . . . well, before this goes any further. Okay?"

Chad sat back and nodded. An instant later, Pepsi jumped into his lap. "Okay."

A shy smile pulled at her lips. "I wasn't a big fan of pretending to be your girlfriend in the beginning." She laughed self-consciously as she ran her fingers over the emerald. "Actually, I was pretty pissed about the whole thing, but it's not like that anymore. I mean . . ." She trailed off, flushing. "God, I sound like an idiot."

Chad tried to hide his smile. "What? You're telling me you didn't agree to do this to increase your dating pool?" he teased.

The flush spread down her throat. "Oh God, no, that's not why I agreed."

Admittedly curious why she had, he idly scratched Pepsi behind his ear. "Tell the truth, you always wanted to be my girlfriend."

Bridget laughed so loud Pepsi lifted his head and flattened his ears. "No. That's not it, either. Miss Gore . . . Well, in a way, I guess I have to thank her for her disturbing level of determination."

His fingers stilled on Pepsi's head. "What do you mean?"

"Miss Gore basically blackmailed me." She reached over, scratching Pepsi's paw. "She threatened to tell people that I was stalking you. She also found out I had been late on my student loans at some point and offered to pay off the debt. You're at least worth fifty thousand, did you know that?" She laughed as Pepsi made bread on Chad's thigh. "I say you're worth more, but—"

"Wait," he said, staring at her. He couldn't believe what he was hearing. "She offered to pay off your student loans to pretend to be my girlfriend."

Bridget nodded. "Yeah, can you believe that?"

Out of the reasons why he'd come up with, the fact that Bridget had been *paid* was not one of them. Shock rippled through him. He didn't know what to feel. Angry? Disappointed? Disgusted?

Bridget was paid to be his girlfriend.

Just like the women that his father paid to be his girlfriend.

A short laugh escaped him as he stared at Bridget. "You know, maybe I was stupid for thinking the reason why you agreed to do this was because you liked me or that you wanted to make up for leaving my ass in the bathroom when we first met."

Confusion poured into Bridget's expression. "Yeah, that would be pretty stupid if you thought that."

"Wow. Okay." Chad picked up Pepsi and sat the very disgruntled cat on the sofa. He stood, hands shaking. "I hope you and Miss Gore are happy with your agreement."

"What?" Bridget shot to her feet. "Chad, wait a second. You can't be that mad."

"I can't be that mad?" He stared at her, incredulous. "Yeah, you know, I've done some pretty fucked-up stuff in my past and a lot of people probably don't think I have a lot of standards, but I do. That's the fucking limit for me. It's disgusting."

She jerked back as if he'd slapped her. After everything, he wasn't even going to give her two seconds to explain she didn't take the money? Was it that easy to believe she'd whore herself out? "Excuse me?"

"This is over."

"Chad!" Bridget moved forward as if to block his escape, but one look from him had her thinking twice. She took a step back, blinking her eyes rapidly. "I don't understand why you won't hear my side."

Chad wasn't sure what he thought, but the truth had never crossed his mind. When money was involved, you could never trust the outcome or anyone's actions.

Shaking his head, he headed for the door. "Your services are no longer needed. This shit is over. I'm done."

Chapter Twenty-one

Bridget was still in a numb daze when she returned to work two days after Christmas. She had no idea how or why Chad had reacted as strongly as he did. She'd just wanted to have all their cards on the table, so to speak, if things had any hope of moving further . . . going beyond pretend. For a moment there, she'd really thought he wanted something real with her and she couldn't go further without the truth between them.

During those two days, she went through every emotional stage and when anger finally showed its ugly head, she'd been grateful. Cussing Chad was better than burying her head in her tear-soaked pillows.

Had he really believed she'd just go out with him because he was that damn awesome? For fuck sake, his ego knew no limits.

But the anger didn't hang around long, and she really shouldn't have been surprised that she was going to work using a ton of concealer under her swollen eyes.

Her heart was broken, just ahead of schedule.

She turned her computer on and listlessly started checking her e-mails. Fifteen minutes later, Madison bounded into the office with a smile so huge Bridget had to wonder if she won the lottery over the break.

Or if Chase had proposed to her.

But Madison's smile faded the moment she saw Bridget. "Oh no, what has happened?"

Bridget wasn't sure if she should tell Madison now that she and Chad were broken up. The last thing she wanted to do was ruin his contract, so she opted for a lie. "I'm not feeling well."

Madison stopped in front of her desk, a look of sympathy crossing her face. "You look like crap."

"Thanks," she muttered.

"But you need to feel better before the third because guess what?" Of course Madison didn't wait for Bridget to guess. Not that she ever did. "Director Bernstein changed his mind. He wants you at the Gala."

"What?" Bridget turned away from her computer. "But he didn't want me—"

"I know, because of Chad, but he's even okay if Chad comes." Madison rocked back on her heels, happy as can be while Bridget's heart cracked a little more. "At first I thought someone pulled the stick out of his ass, but then he shared even bigger news, which is why he's in such a great mood."

"What?" Viagra no longer posed heart attack risks?

Madison slapped her hands down on Bridget's desk, rattling every item on it. "There was a *generous* donation that came in after Christmas."

Despite her craptastic mood, hope swelled. "How generous?"

"Generous as in we have met our goal for the year!"

Bridget shot to her feet. "Are you serious?"

"Yes!" Madison jumped. "The department has their funding for the year, and there are still some donations expected to be made at the Gala!"

Rushing around the desk, Bridget joined Madison in the jumping and squealing celebration. Her mood most definitely approved upon hearing the good news, which helped get her through the day. There were only a few times the stuff with Chad overshadowed the good, but she kept telling herself at least she didn't have to worry about finding a new job for another year.

It was when she returned home that evening and set Pepsi's dinner on the table, she almost broke down again.

Tears never solved anything, but she wanted to cave to them. Right now, she had so much to look forward to, but it had lost a little of its luster.

A knock on her door had her heart stopping. Was it Chad? She'd called and texted him several times, wanting a chance to explain, to talk, to do something, but he hadn't responded.

She rushed through the living room, catching her toe in the threadbare carpet, nearly face-planting into the floor. Catching herself at the last minute, she threw open the door. "Cha . . . oh, it's you."

Miss Gore arched a brow. "Nice to see you, too."

Well, if she hadn't felt like crawling into a hole before, now she did. "What do you want?"

"We need to talk." She pushed her way into Bridget's apartment. For someone so small, she was definitely strong. Turning around, Miss Gore placed her purse on the coffee table and folded her arms. "Can you tell me why I just got off the phone with a really pissy Chad, who just explained to me that the whole thing was off, ahead of schedule, and will not tell me why?"

Bridget's shoulders slumped. "It's over."

Her eyes narrowed. "What do you mean? We weren't planning to break things off—"

"There isn't any 'we' in this! And I don't care if this messes up everything for you!" She stepped back, taking a deep breath. "Look, I want Chad to keep his contract and for everything to work out for him, but it's over."

Miss Gore watched her a moment and then sat down. "What happened?"

"Why do you think something happened?"

"Because you're hurt," she said, taking off her glasses. "I can tell. It's in your eyes. So I imagine something happened. And we planned to call this off after New Year's. And that is still a few days away."

Bridget couldn't even believe she was considering telling her the truth, but she sat down, shaking her head slowly. "I'm in love with him."

Miss Gore sat back.

"And I think . . . Well, I thought he felt the same way." Tears crawled up her throat. "But I screwed up. I told him the truth."

"The truth about what?" she asked. "The student loans? Look, I know that's a sore spot with you, obviously, but it's not that big of a deal. I doubt Chad—"

"No." Bridget sighed. "I told him why I agreed to do this."

Miss Gore paled. "Oh, dear . . ."

"I told him that I hadn't wanted to and that you basically blackmailed me." She pursed her lips. "By the way, don't think I'm not still pissed off by that. I am."

She nodded. "Understandable. And he was mad?"

"Mad?" Bridget let out a short, humorless laugh that just sounded really sad. "He was beyond pissed. He walked right out."

Miss Gore raised one brow. "Well, I imagine it doesn't do wonders for a man's ego, especially one of his size, to hear a woman agreed to be his girlfriend because she was blackmailed. Have you tried calling him?"

Pressing her lips together, Bridget nodded. The ball of ugh was in her throat and going nowhere. "I've called. I've texted. He hasn't responded."

Her brows puckered. Several moments passed. "I do believe he's developed strong feelings for you—possibly even love."

Bridget scowled. "What part of the conversation do you not understand? He left. He doesn't want to see me. That's not love."

The publicist smiled. "The only reason why he'd be mad is because he has feelings. If he didn't, he wouldn't have cared. The fact that he is upset proves that he has feelings." She leaned forward, patting her hand. Bridget jerked back, but Miss Gore was nonplussed. "This is good—great. I couldn't have dared to hope for a real relationship to come out of this, but this is perfect. People will be clamoring to hire me."

"You're insane," Bridget said, staring at her.

"No. You just wait and see. He'll come around." She stood, smiling like she just had the best year at work. "You know, I was starting to suspect something." She clapped her hands together. "You will end up thanking me for this."

Bridget's mouth dropped open. "Get out of my apartment."

"I'm serious." She picked up her purse. "In the end, you'll invite me to the wedding, and you'll thank me in the toast."

In total shock, Bridget did the same thing she had done the first time Miss Gore visited her apartment.

Bridget flipped her off.

With both hands.

Chad was in a funk or, how his brothers put it, PMSing. He hadn't told them what went down between him and Bridget. It wasn't any of their business.

His feet pounded on the treadmill. He'd been running for the last hour. Sweat poured from him. Every night since he discovered the truth behind why Bridget had readily agreed to be his pretend girlfriend, he'd spent more hours on the treadmill than he cared to count.

Muscles burned an unholy fire, but it was better than the cold cavern in his chest. It was better than sitting in front of the TV not really paying attention to the screen. And it was far better than lying in bed staring at his ceiling, wondering how in the fuck he had misjudged Bridget so badly.

He slowed down and then smacked the stop button. He got off the treadmill and ripped the towel from the arm and started mopping up his sweat.

Then again, how fucking stupid was he that he really thought she'd go along with this just because of *who* he was? Even he could admit that his ego had surpassed all of his brothers' combined—and his father's.

Maybe he could one day understand why she did it, but he could never get past it. Not when his father did shit like that, buying his "girlfriends" jewels, cars, paying off debt, and furnishing their apartments while his mother doped herself into an early grave.

And what the hell was he thinking, anyway? Him in a relationship—one that had started off by two people pretending to be in love? Shit, he was worse than his father when it came to his track record with women.

Fuck.

But he missed Bridget's smile—her laugh. He missed how she always smelled of jasmine and the way she felt against him. He missed the blush that always popped up on her face and traveled down her neck.

Chad missed the witty comebacks and the way she was okay when things were quiet. He missed her asking about his day and hating the paparazzi and the way she never let him get away with anything. He even missed that fat-ass cat of hers.

He just fucking missed her.

Dropping the towel, he then ran his hands down his face. Avoiding the calls had been hard enough, but not reaching out to her had been a real effort. He was about to hop in the shower when he heard a knock on the front door. Figuring it was one of his brothers trying to drag him out for New Year's and ignoring the rush of excitement at the thought it might be Bridget, he answered the door.

It was worse.

"Miss Gore." He drew her name out, the way he knew she hated. "What did I do to earn this pleasure?"

She scowled as her gaze drifted over him. "Do you ever wear a shirt when you're home?"

"No. If you have a problem, see you—"

She put her hand up, stopping his attempt to close the door in her face. "I wouldn't have to be coming here if you would answer your phone and stop acting like a general ass."

Chad closed his eyes and counted to ten. "Like I said in the last phone call, I don't need your services anymore. You did your job. Congrats and thank you. Now please get the hell out of my life."

Miss Gore pushed past him, went into his kitchen, and hopped up on the bar stool and crossed her legs. "I'm still your publicist until the Nationals decide my services are no longer needed."

"Great," he muttered.

"And you do need me."

Chad grabbed a bottle of water and propped his hip against the counter. "You're the last person I need."

"Okay." She smiled. "You need Bridget."

A sharp pain hit him in the gut. "I stand corrected. She's the last person I need."

"Really?" she replied. "Then if she was the last person you needed, why did you sleep with her?"

Chad swore under his breath. "I'm not talking—"

"Oh, you'll talk to me, all right." Miss Gore spun on the stool, tracking his movements. "You shouldn't have slept with her if you were going to turn around and walk out!"

"Why are you upset? You set this whole damn thing up!" Chad was dumbfounded. "What did you think was going to happen?"

"Oh, I don't know." Miss Gore folded her arms. "That you actually got over yourself? So what? She didn't want to date you in the beginning—she needed a little push."

Chad was about to throw this woman out of his apartment. "You blackmailed her into being with me."

"I didn't blackmail her into sleeping with you, you big dumbass!"

"Yeah, you're paying her to do so." Chad smirked. "Big fucking difference there."

"What?" Miss Gore sat back and let out a laugh. "You're an idiot."

"First off, I don't think any of this is funny and secondly—"

"Yes. You're an idiot." Miss Gore shot to her feet, planting her hands on her hips. "Let me guess.

Bridget started explaining to you why she agreed to do this, but you heard only what your sensitive male ears wanted to hear and jumped to conclusions? Because I didn't pay Bridget a dime for doing this."

"That's not—"

"I did offer to pay her—to pay off her student loans, to be exact. I thought that would be a better incentive," Miss Gore said. "And after dealing with you for less than a month, I figured we needed to pay the poor girl."

Wow. Chad set the bottle down. "Well, that's unnecessary."

"But Bridget refused the money, which forced me to take more drastic steps. Trust me, I'm not proud of what I did, but Bridget has done nothing wrong. I gave her no choice in this."

Chad thrust his fingers through his hair and turned, breathing in deeply. "She turned down the money?"

"Yes."

"And you forced her to do this?"

"Yes," she replied. "But whatever happened between you had nothing to do with me. That was all you two."

Chad closed his eyes as a rush of mixed-up emotions hammered inside him. He didn't know what to think. Relief poured through him, but so did anger—mostly at himself. Miss Gore was right. His overinflated ego had gotten the best of him.

"It's not too late."

He faced her. "Yeah, I think it's too late."

"Why?"

"How can anything come from a relationship that started off because someone was forced into it?"

Miss Gore threw her hands up. "Look, you've spent your whole life never accepting responsibility for anything you do. It's always everyone else's fault. But here is the one chance for you to realize you had something to do with this. And do I need to remind you that you had a relationship with her before I stepped in? I just helped it along."

"Helped it?"

She nodded, smiling. "Do you love her?"

"I . . ."

"It's an easy question, Chad. Do you love her?"

The answer was easy. His heart already knew what his mouth didn't want to say. For some reason, he thought about the damn playground, saw his life going round and round but never really ending up anywhere—or with anyone. It was time to get off the merry-go-round.

"If you do," she said firmly, "you will find a way to fix this."

Chad stared at his publicist/babysitter/daughter of Satan. "Jesus, woman, I do not envy the man you end up with."

Miss Gore's smile was pure evil. "Neither do I."

Chapter Twenty-two

It was only an hour into the Winter Fund-raiser Gala, and her face hurt from all the smiling and her feet were killing her from avoiding Robert and Madison.

Really not fair for Madison, but she had Chase with her, and besides, the fact that he looked so much like Chad was a little bit disturbing. Plus he immediately wanted to know what the hell crawled up Chad's ass since Christmas.

It hurt to even think about answering that, and she knew she would have to eventually once Miss Gore gave up on the idea of Chad coming around. Their very real breakup of their very fake relationship would go public soon.

Bridget tried not to think about that as she greeted guests and kept track of the caterers. She was pretty sure one of them was high as a kite. She was torn between asking the kid to leave and finding out where he hid his stash.

Director Bernstein approached her with a warm smile and clasped her hands in his. "The Gala is amazing, Miss Rodgers. You and Miss Daniels have outdone yourselves this year."

"Thank you. I hope we can have the same turnout next year."

The skin around his eyes crinkled. "Well, as long as that boyfriend of yours is around, I'm sure we will."

Bridget blinked slowly. "Come again?"

Patting her on the shoulder, he laughed softly. "There's no need for pretense. I know Mr. Gamble asked me to keep his donation a secret, but I'm sure he had to have shared his act of generosity with you."

Her stomach dropped.

"Because of him, the volunteer department will see another year, probably two." Director Bernstein squeezed her shoulder, but she really didn't feel it. "I shouldn't have been so quick to cut him out. After all that he has done for the Institute, he should be here."

"Uh . . ." Bridget had no idea what to say.

The director gave her another squeeze. "Enjoy yourself tonight. You deserve it. And please pass along my gratitude to Mr. Gamble."

Bridget nodded dumbly and watched Director Bernstein rejoin his wife. Several moments passed before it fully sank in.

Chad had made the last donation that might not have saved the department all on its own, but it had saved her job and was what had gotten her reinvited to her own event. Hope and confusion battled it out for top contender for what she was feeling right now. Obviously, he'd done this before he'd found out she had been conned into being his girlfriend. Right?

Dodging guests, she found Madison with Chase. "Did you know?" she blurted out.

Madison's eyes widened. "Did I know what?"

"Did you know that Chad had been the one who made the donation that took us to our goal?"

"What?" She turned to Chase, smacking him in the arm. Hard. "You didn't tell me?"

Okay. Madison really didn't know.

"Hey." Chase held up his hands. "I have no idea what you're talking about."

"Oh my God," Bridget said, stunned. "I can't believe he made that donation. That was so much money."

"Damn," Chase said, brows raised. "I don't think Chad has ever made a donation to anything except when he plays poker, because he's sure to lose. The Smithsonian should name a room after him."

Madison grinned. "Actually, they should name it after Bridget, because I'm sure that's why he made the donation."

Turning around, Bridget smoothed her hands over the skirt of her simple black dress. She had to do something. She didn't know what or if it changed a damn thing, but she had to thank him.

Bridget had to ask him why.

Spinning back to Madison, she took a deep breath. "I . . . I have to go."

"What?" Madison stepped forward. "Bridget, are you—"

"I'm okay. Really." She paused to smile at Chase. "I just need to go, okay?"

Whirling around, she didn't wait for Madison or Chase to say anything else. She cut across the main room, hastily delving out smiles and kept going so she couldn't be stopped.

She was ten feet from the entrance when she came to a complete stop and the air rushed out of her lungs.

Standing under the twinkling white lights was Chad Gamble.

He was dressed in a tux, dressed like he'd planned on attending, and God, he looked wonderful. His sky blue eyes scanned the room and landed on her.

She couldn't move. The world around her ceased to exist.

With a look of determination, he strode toward her. He didn't walk. Oh no, he stalked up to her.

"Going somewhere?" he asked.

"Yes." She shook her head. "I was leaving to find you."

"You were?" He cocked his head to the side. "Why?"

"I need to talk to you." She glanced around as she took ahold of his arm, hoping to move the conversation to a much more private area. "You made the donation."

Bridget couldn't glean anything from his expression, and he wasn't moving. "I did," he replied.

"Why?" She kept her voice low. "Chad, that was so much money and—"

"I love you," he said, and loud enough that several people around them stopped and turned. A bit of blush filled the hollows of his cheeks. "That's why I did it. May not have fully realized it at the time, but I do. I love you. And I can't have my girl not having her job."

Bridget stared at him, unsure she heard him correctly, but by then, they had gained such an audience and, by the expressions on their faces, they had to have imagined the same thing.

"You love me?" she squeaked out.

A half smile appeared. "Yeah, I do."

Everything felt surreal, like she was dreaming. "Maybe we should go talk somewhere—"

"No. I want to do this here," he said, dropping his hands on her shoulders. "I've been an ass the majority of my life. I didn't want to get off the playground, you know."

"What?"

He shook his head. "Forget the playground statement but listen. From the night I first met you, I knew I was never going to meet another woman like you. I should've found you after then, but somehow you came back into my life. I don't know how. I really don't deserve that kind of luck, and I sure as hell don't deserve a woman like you."

Tears were building in her eyes. "Chad . . ."

"I'm not finished, babe." His blue eyes were dancing. "I've done a lot of things I'm not proud of. I didn't sleep with those women, by the way. Still didn't do that, but that's not the point. I did do a lot of things that impacted other people. I never took responsibility for any of it, but what I regret most was leaving your place on Christmas Day."

Oh God, she was going to start bawling. "Chad, it's okay. We can—"

"It wasn't okay. I should've heard you out." He let go, taking a deep breath. "And I never wanted to fix anything until now, and it has nothing to do with the contract. Fuck the contract."

Bridget sucked in a breath, but it got caught.

"I want to fix things because of you. I want to be worthy of you."

Tears sneaked out of her eyes then. "But you are, Chad. You are."

A bit of the smugness eked into his expression. "Well, I know I'm great, but I could be better for you."

Bridget laughed shakily. "Wow."

"What I'm trying to say is that you're the best fake girlfriend I've ever had." Chad went down on one knee in front of her and the entire world. "I'm in awe of you."

She froze. "What are you doing?"

"Holy shit," Chase said from the sidelines.

"Shut up," hissed Madison.

Chad shot his brother a wicked look and then turned his gaze back to her. "This may be crazy, but what the hell, right?" He reached into his pocket and pulled out a small black box, and Bridget felt faint as he cracked it open. An emerald set in a silver band winked up at her. "I love you, Bridget. I'm pretty sure you feel the same way about me, and screw the whole dating thing. Let's get married."

Blood drained from her upper body so fast she really thought she was going to topple right over.

Chad waited. "What do you say? Will you marry me?"

Oddly enough, Bridget's entire life flashed before her eyes. Which was really weird, considering she wasn't dying or anything, but it did. In an instant, everything she had ever been and ever would be collided. Her heart swelled. Happiness rushed over her.

Her eyes locked with his and the words came out. "Yes. Yes!"

There was a thunderous roar as Chad rose to his feet and slipped the ring on. It was a little big, but she couldn't care about that in the moment. Looking up at Chad, she closed her eyes as his lips descended on hers in the sweetest, most tender kiss they ever shared.

"Holy shit," she heard Chase say again, and Chad and her parted, laughing as they saw his dumbstruck brother standing next to Madison.

Wrapping his arms around Bridget, Chad lowered his mouth to her ear. "Thank you," he said. "Thank you."

She burrowed her face into his neck as she clutched his arms. "You do deserve me."

He slid his arms to her waist. "Then show me."

She so got what he was referencing. Grabbing Chad by the arm, she shot the director an apologetic smile. "Sorry about the circus. Really, I am."

Director Bernstein looked as stunned as she felt, but she kept going, leading Chad out into the lobby and down the hall. They made a pit stop in the first room they found—a small storage room holding the wine for the Gala. It was chilled in there, but it was perfect.

Chad locked the door behind him and turned to her, eyes flaring a deep blue. "I need to hear you say it."

Her heart fluttered. "I love you, Chad. I wanted to tell you that on Christmas, but—"

"But I acted like a douche, I know." He came up to her and reached up, tugging her hair down so it was a mess of waves and curls. "I want to spend the rest of my life making up for it."

Amazing how those words turned her on more than anything in this world. "Then start making up for it now."

"Oh, I like that. Bossy pants." His head dipped and he

kissed her—kissed her in a way that was so different from before, as if he was telling her that he knew he had her, and he was never letting go. "Think you can handle marrying a player?"

Bridget slid her hand between them, finding where he was already ready for her. "As long as he's a player only on the field, yes." She cupped him and smiled when he moaned against her lips. "You think you can handle me?"

In a split second, Chad had her flipped around, her back pressed against his front. "What do you think?" His breath was hot in her ear as he slid a hand up her thigh. "No stockings. I have to say I agree."

Her panties were gone before she could even say a word. They ended up down by her ankles and she stepped out of them.

"That's my girl." He kissed the back of her neck. "That's my soon-to-be wife."

The sound of his zipper coming down almost had her coming right then. There was no other warning. He slid into her, his rhythm hot and furious, relentless and beautiful, as he guided her neck back, bringing his mouth to hers. Both were panting, their hips rocking into each other as he took them to a soul-shattering release that left them breathless.

When Chad spun her around to face him, he kissed her deeply and held her against him, every so often dropping a kiss to her cheek and then her eyelids.

"I guess I do have to thank Miss Gore," Bridget admitted when she could speak again.

"What for?" Chad straightened the hem on her dress and then pressed a kiss to her throat.

She smiled up at him, her heart swelling so fast she was sure it was going to burst. "For you."

Chad cupped her cheeks. "You're right, but I'm the one who needs to be thanking her. She brought *you* back into my life. Let's never tell her though," he said, kissing her lips. "She can come to the wedding, but God knows her head can't get any bigger. She doesn't need our help."

Bridget laughed as she looped her arms around Chad's neck, happier than she ever believed possible—with Chad Gamble of all people, a player on the field and a reformed one off. And all because of the publicist from hell. Funny how things worked out.

"Agreed," she said, smiling.

Chad dipped his head once more and based on the way he was kissing her, taking her into him over and over again, they wouldn't be leaving the wine room anytime soon.

Acknowledgments

A special thank-you goes out to Liz Pelletier and the team behind Entangled Brazen for loving the Gamble Brothers as much as I do, and to Kevan Lyon for being the awesomesauce agent that she always is. And to my publicist Stacey O'Neale, thank you for all the hard work you do. Thank you to my friends who've always been a huge support—Stacey Morgan, Dawn, Lesa, Cindy, and so on—and to my family and husband.

None of this would be possible without all you readers out there. I owe you the biggest thanks in the world. Every one of you amazes me. Thank you.

TEMPTING THE BODYGUARD

9781473615953

He can protect her from everyone except himself…

Alana Gore is in danger. A take-no-prisoners publicist, her way with people has made her more than a few enemies over the years, but a creepy stalker is an entirely different matter. She needs a bodyguard, and the only man she can ask is not only ridiculously hot, but reputed to have taste for women that goes beyond adventurous.

Chandler Gamble has one rule: don't protect anyone you want to screw. But with Alana, he's caught between his job and his increasingly hard libido. On one hand, Alana needs his help. On the other, Chandler wants nothing more than to take the hot volcano of a woman in hand. To make her writhe in pleasure, until she's at his complete mercy.

She needs protection. He needs satisfaction. And the moment the line is crossed, all hell will break loose...

Available now in ebook, coming soon in paperback

HODDER